CW00486523

ELITE STARFIGHTER

STARFIGHTER TRAINING ACADEMY - GAME 3

GRACE GOODWIN

GET A FREE BOOK!

http://freescifiromance.com

1

arius, Moon Base Arturri, in orbit around Planet Velerion

I STOOD in the entrance to our newly assigned private quarters and watched Lily Wilson of Earth open one of the heavy cases she'd insisted we bring along. My pair-bonded female had been prepared and waiting for my arrival on Earth with five large cases stacked and waiting to go. Thinking I would need to introduce myself, explain about the training protocols, and seduce her, if necessary, to convince her to come back to Velerion with me, I'd been shocked when she'd opened her door, said my name, and shoved one of the cases toward me.

No argument. No questions. She'd simply said, *"Darius. About time. Let's go."* Not exactly the welcome I'd been hoping for. No gasp of surprise. No inspection or questions. No touching or locked gazes. No kissing. Taking. Claiming.

Nothing to give away her thoughts or her mood. She was like a wall of ice, and I had yet to find a single crack in her composure.

"What are you doing? The general said to rest. Jamie and Mia cannot meet with you until tomorrow." General Aryk had been the highest-ranking official on the base when I'd arrived with Lily. He'd insisted we rest and informed us they were still cleaning up after a large operation to take back the planet Xenon and its moon base from Queen Raya and the Dark Fleet. They'd been successful, but there were still pockets of resistance on the surface keeping everyone busy. Including Lily's friends, Mia and Jamie, the two additional Earth females who had earned Elite Starfighter ranks.

Lily glanced up at my question, looked from the bed to me, and hastily averted her gaze. "I'm not tired. And I want to unpack."

Watching her now, I held back a groan as she leaned forward, the curves of her breasts taunting me where her clothing dipped low. Lily was softness and curves. Golden-brown hair, green and gold eyes. She was supposed to be mine. To fight beside me. To care about our war with the Xandraxians and Queen Raya. I hoped she would be eager to climb inside the Elite Starfighter Titan in which she would battle. Yet here she was, in the Vega Star System, twenty-five light-years from her former life, and she had not touched me. Had spoken my name only once. In fact, she only seemed to care about finding her two human friends.

To say I was confused would be an understatement. During our training simulations, Lily had been savage in battle, cursing in more languages than I could recall as she pounded enemies into dust.

I had expected Lily to be raw, fearless, her emotions and needs exposed. Instead I could not read her at all. She was like a wild animal hiding behind fortified walls. Watching me. Waiting. But for what? I had no experience with human females except her. And she was not behaving as I had expected. Perhaps I needed to try another tactic.

"What is in those cases? Stones?"

"Books."

"What are books?" Lily's body had successfully accepted the cipher implant injection, and we had been conversing, if awkwardly, the entire trip from Earth. Still, I did not know this term.

She opened the case, and I crouched to inspect the strange rectangular objects layered four or five deep inside. They appeared to be oddly thin sheets of parchment or canvas stacked and wrapped in thicker bits that covered the outside. They were made of many different colors and what I assumed were human names on the outside. The labels indicated topics ranging from war to philosophy to animals. One caught my eye as it appeared to have a human pair bond engaged in some sort of mating ritual on the cover.

I grabbed the book, barely evading her attempt to swat my hand away. Now I was extremely interested in the contents. Holding the image this way and that to inspect it, I rose and walked over to lean my shoulder against the wall, giving her a bit of distance. She was jumpy. Nervous. Always on edge.

Her anxiety made me want to wrap my arms around her and hold her until she melted in my arms. Until she was mine.

"What are these books?" I asked again. "And why did you bring so many?"

She sighed and began removing the remaining books, placing them in stacks on the floor beside her, sorting them in some mysterious way only she understood.

"They're stories written by people and immortalized on paper. Some of these are hundreds of years old."

That was the most Lily had said to me since I'd stood before her and told her who I was. I thumbed through the parchment I held. "This will burn quite easily. How does this make the story immortal?"

Rubbing her palms over her blue jean–covered thighs, she tugged the sleeve of her hoodie—which was decorated with the logo of her favorite university team—higher on her arm. Earth clothing appeared to be soft and not very functional, and those were all words I had learned in the last few hours. She looked up at me with a plea in her eyes and held out her hand. "It doesn't matter. Just give that back, please."

Please? Had she just said *please*?

Unable to deny her, I walked to her and placed the book in her outstretched hand. She took the item and twisted to place it behind her on the floor as I lifted another, similar looking book from the case, surprised to note there were six or seven more stacked beneath this one. All with the same name on the books' sides.

"Darius!" Lily's cheeks turned an interesting shade of pink.

"Yes?" Interesting indeed. This book had a human name at the bottom of the thick cover. "Grace Goodwin. *Her Cyborg Beast*? The Colony?" I turned the rectangle over and absorbed the meaning of the words that covered the back side. I considered the ideas, wondering if my cipher implant was malfunctioning. "Mated means pair-bonded? For life?"

"Yes." Lily lifted her hand to her face and covered her eyes. "Just give that back. Don't worry about it."

"Interstellar Brides? A colony? I did not know Earth had entered into any treaties or trade agreements with other worlds." Was Velerion intelligence wrong about the small blue planet? Had Earth's people made pacts we were unaware of?

"We haven't. It's fiction, okay? Make-believe."

"Make me believe what, exactly?"

"It's just a story. Imagination. None of it is true. It's for entertainment. That's all."

"Interesting."

"Not really. Just give it back."

"Not yet." I very much wanted to open this book and

discover what human stories said of pair bonds and mating rituals.

With an irritated grumble, Lily apparently decided her best course of action was to ignore me and devote her undivided attention to unpacking her cases and cases of books.

Which left me time to wonder at the *entertainment* I held in my hand. Lily appeared to be entertained by large males with bulging muscles and biosynthetic implants just below the skin. On the outside covering of the book, the male's expression was serious and the words on the back spoke of war and torture. A beast of some kind.

Hoping to understand Lily a bit, I opened the book to a random page and began to read. The time I had spent in training simulations with Lily had accustomed my cipher implant to reading in her language. However, the words shocked me. Made my body react with need. Lust. Desire. Everything I'd been fighting diligently to control since the moment I met Lily came roaring to life as the *Beast* man in the story boldly told his human female exactly what he would do to her body. The ways he would claim her. Fill her with his seed. Make her body writhe with pleasure. Pound his hard cock into her wet heat and make her come over and over...

The book fell from my hands and landed with a soft *thud* on the floor.

Fuck. *This* was what Lily had brought with her from Earth? Not clothing. Sentimental items. Jewelry. No.

Lily had books full of hot, naked sex? Dominant

males seducing their pair-bonded females? Fucking. Tasting. Claiming them for all time. The story had been told in the female's perspective as her mate had filled her body with his cock. Pumped into her. Touched her. Kissed her. The lust burning from the pages had me struggling to breathe.

"Lily?"

"Yes?" Her clipped tone held little to no interest in my presence. She had moved on from organizing her books on the floor to placing them in groups inside the cabinets along the bedroom wall. As she'd done from the moment her wide eyes had landed on me with shock when I appeared at her door for the first time, she appeared to be doing anything and everything she could to ignore me.

This human female had already wrecked my carefully laid plan. Ruined everything. Nothing she did was expected. I had no idea what to say to her or how to approach her.

How to get her naked.

She'd barely spoken to me, but fuck all that was holy, she started humming as she went about the room, organizing her things, her soft, lilting voice going straight to my hard cock.

"Is that what you desire?"

"What are you talking about?" Her movements became quick once again. Stilted.

"The beast man in that story of yours. He took his female and held her against the wall, filled her with his cock. Made her scream with release."

"Oh, bloody hell," she whispered under her breath but would not look at me.

"Lily? Answer me. Is. That. What. You. Want?" Because I was fully capable, eager, to take her against the wall and make her scream. But the only name she would be calling out would be mine.

My name. Over and over. Until she knew exactly who had claimed her.

2

OH, shit. I should have left my romance novels at home. But when considering the rest of my life, I only wanted to read *Wuthering Heights* or *Odyssey* so many times. The classics were, well, classic, and I'd brought along hundreds, if not thousands of dollars' worth of books, but I knew I would want something fun to read. Sexy. Stories that made me happy when I turned the last page.

The rest of my life was a long damn time.

And now Darius was looking at me like he was a hungry lion and I was dinner.

"Lily?" He walked toward me, pulled me to my feet with gentle hands until I faced him. I wanted to look away, but the slightest touch of his fingers on my cheek and I was frozen in place.

"Darius." I was drowning in his eyes. Drowning. My heart pounded, my legs were shaking.

"I asked you a question, Titan."

Titan? Was I a Titan? One of the biggest, baddest tech warriors in the Starfighter program? Six meters of walking, talking, destruction? Truly?

Perhaps I was all those things in a game...no, not a game, a training program I'd *believed* was nothing more than a video game back on Earth, *Starfighter Training Academy.* Sitting in my living room behind a controller, I was unhinged. Fearless. But in the flesh? Real tough I was turning out to be. A real lady, too. Ladies did not want the things I imagined Darius doing to me. And what now? How could I tell him I wanted to try everything I'd read in my beast books, but I'd never been with anyone before.

"I should finish unpacking," I whispered, staring at his lips. Why couldn't I just say yes? Why? Need was a living, burning beast within, but I choked on the word.

I had been raised to be respectful and quiet. Demure. A lady looked after the needs of others before herself. My mother had taught me to never let my guard down with a man. Never trust. "*Use every asset at your disposal to get what you want,*" she'd once said to me, "*but don't ever give a man your heart.*"

I'd watched my father's stoic indifference break my mother into a thousand tiny pieces. I'd watched her try to drink herself into not caring. But she loved him anyway.

Still did, for all I knew. They usually sent an email with photos from a new exotic locale every few months, my father busy with "work" and my mother amusing herself with "lessons" at the Country Club or the latest resort. I'd learned early on this was my mother's prim and proper code for *fucking whatever they could, wherever they could*. My mother would never be so crass as to say the word fuck, but that's what she meant. It had almost become a game to them. A competition.

I didn't want any part of it, and so I had steered clear of men. In all honesty, foraging around for a penis to take my virginity hadn't seemed worth the effort when a discreet, electronic toy gave me perfectly acceptable orgasms with none of the drama. After one disastrous dating montage in college, I had learned to ignore men. All men, except digital versions who couldn't break my heart.

If I didn't want to get involved with men then standing here in front of the live version of the man I had literally built from the ground up in the game, every detail of my partner chosen from the dark, sexy voice to his hotter than hell body and cocky, dominant personality was all kinds of wrong. Big mistake. Darius of was a real, flesh and blood Velerion who had spent hours filling out questionnaires and surveys in order to create the game version of himself, all in the hopes of being selected by a Starfighter. Selected by someone like me. My perfect partner, and he had heartbreak written all over him in bold, capital letters. Crazy, but I'd fallen for him long before I knew he was real. If I let him touch me the way his eyes said he wanted to, there would be no going back.

Not that my body was listening to a hint of common sense. My nipples hardened into aching pebbles. My core was tight and pulsing and so very empty. I wanted him to pound into me like a beast.

"Lily, talk to me."

The air left my body in a whoosh, and I licked suddenly dry lips, my tongue brushing the tip of his finger. He stared, taking the opportunity to slowly stroke my damp bottom lip with his thumb. I lifted my hand to his chest and settled it above his heart. "I don't want to talk."

His turn to stop breathing.

My words were honest. The absolute truth. I didn't want to talk. I didn't want to lay my soul bare or ask him for anything. I sure as hell didn't want to tell him the only knob I'd ever handled had been battery powered. Playing by the rules had done nothing but earned me a lonely, dead-end job at a library so old it smelled like a morgue for books. Most days I was the youngest person in the building by an average of two decades. I loved books, loved the classics, but I was tired of reading about adventures and never having one of my own.

Darius, tall, dark, sexy Darius was standing in front of me looking at me like he wanted to rip my clothes off. I was on another planet. Earth Lily was dead now. I didn't have to behave like her another moment.

Starfighter Lily Wilson could be the Titan Darius had

named me. I could be brave and sexy and wild. Powerful. Fearless. Important. Adored.

Could I not?

If I were so brave and sexy and wild, why did my heart threaten to pound its way out from behind my rib cage? Why did I feel like I was about to faint? My body drifted and swayed like whispers and smoke, the only thing anchoring me to reality the heat of Darius's thumb on my lip.

I watched as he lowered his head slowly, his gaze moving at the last moment from my eyes to my lips. So, so close. The heat of his breath was like fire in my throat as I soaked him in. His scent. His desire.

Nothing existed but us. Time stopped. We drifted toward one another.

Contact.

His lips were firm. Hot. Demanding.

That was the end of me. I lost my bloody mind.

"Off. Off. Off." I tugged at his clothing, the soft black clothing he'd changed into when we'd been shown to our new quarters. "Take them off. Now."

Darius didn't answer, but his hands went to the hem of his shirt and tugged it off over his head, breaking our kiss just long enough to pull the fabric from between us before devouring me again.

It wasn't enough.

Reaching down, I pulled my hoodie off over my head, revealing the black spaghetti-strap tank top I wore underneath. Peeking at him from my shoulders were the straps of my hot pink bra, the only sexy bra and knickers set I owned. There was nothing extraordinary about me. I was average in every way—height, bra size, hair color. I was no runway model or stunning beauty. I was just me.

Darius reached for me, his hands settling at my waist as he inspected the close-fitting tank top and flirty pink bra. I stopped breathing as the silence stretched. Tried to pull away.

He stopped me, kissed me again, then pulled me close. Darius lowered his hands to my hips and pulled my lower body into intimate contact with his hard—rock-hard—length, leaving me no doubt that he very much liked what he had seen.

Darius

I KISSED HER, and she pulled away.

I asked her questions. She refused to answer.

What the fuck was I missing here?

"Lily? Talk to me. Tell me what you want."

Silence. A blush to her cheeks. I could barely think straight staring at her lips, feeling the softness of her pressed against me. The taste of her on my tongue. *I* was the one who was supposed to be leading the way between us. This was my planet, my people, my war. Not hers. Just as I was not yet hers, and I fucking wanted to be. Needed to be.

My broken pieces were in the palm of her hand, and she was supposed to glue me back together. I'd found my pair-bonded mate at last. A true pairing. Like minds. Complementary skills. We would forever be better together than apart. I'd spent hundreds of hours fighting next to her in our simulation training, learning her moods and the sound of her voice through the recordings she'd made for her avatar. She *knew* me, yet acted as if we were strangers. As if *I* did not know *her*.

Damn her. Maybe I didn't know her at all. Perhaps I was the fool here.

Her pulse raced at the base of her throat, and she licked her lips. A groan slipped from mine. "Are you ignoring me, or trying to seduce me?" I asked, my tone deliberately neutral.

"I don't know," she countered. "I don't know what I want."

"That is a lie, Lily."

Her gaze shot to mine as she gasped. "What?"

"You heard me. You know what you want. What I don't know is why you won't be honest with me. I am your pair bond. I am yours, Lily. I'm yours until the day I die. Do you understand?"

Her smile was a bit sad. She lifted her hand and pointed to her temple. "Do I understand here?" She lowered her hand to cover her heart. "Or here? They are two very different questions."

"I only have one answer to give you. You're mine."

I'd never taken the jeans off a human female before, but they were easy to strip away. I grunted when I tugged off her panties as well until she was bare from the waist down. She wiggled her hips to help me undress her and actually kicked the jeans away as if they were an annoyance once they were pooled at her feet.

"You are mine, Lily. Your orgasms? They're mine."

I circled her entrance with the lightest touch, teasing her as I stared down into her eyes. I kept my touch brief but deliberate, explored around and around her core so she was squirming, eager to take more.

"Do you want me to shove your back against the wall and take you like a beast would?" I asked, brushing my thumb over her clit, careful to only make her more desperate. She wouldn't be allowed to come. Not yet, not until she understood how things would be between us from this moment on.

"Yes."

At last. An admission. Desire. The truth.

Perhaps she wanted my touch as badly as I needed to touch her.

I claimed her mouth once more, guiding her until her back hit the wall of our bedchamber, and she whimpered in response, her lips molten and wild, her hands frantic, tugging at my clothing.

"Like this?" I lowered my hand to her hip, her ass. Caressed the soft skin there. Lifted her so that her wet heat was where I needed it so I could fill her, take her, make her mine.

Her fingers tangled in my hair, and I moved to kiss the curve of her jaw, her neck. The soft arch of her shoulder. I tugged the tight, black top she wore over her head until her breasts were displayed in a pink contraption that matched the tiny underthings I'd removed with her jeans.

Perhaps I should have left those on.

I pulled the fabric down with my teeth until her lush nipple was on display, and then quickly sucked the taut peak into my mouth.

I moaned as an orgasm drew tight in my balls, threatening to spill from me when she moaned and tugged my hair, and I knew the taste of her skin was already an addiction.

There was no doubt she felt my cock, hot and throbbing against her hip. There was no hiding her effect on me, my desperation. How badly I needed her. I was a Velerion warrior, and yet, she had no idea exactly how much power she would have over me.

"Oh God, Darius," she groaned.

Her deep breathing, her cries of obvious pleasure filled the small room, went straight to my cock.

Holding her up with my left arm, I slipped my right low, to her center and slid two fingers deep. The wet heat of her pulsed and clamped down on the invasion, and she thrust her hips toward me with a sudden jolt. "I want you."

"Not yet. Come for me. Give yourself to me."

"No."

She gasped when I withdrew my touch, then pushed deep. "Yes."

"No. Not like this. I want you inside me."

Fuck.

Was she a weapon sent to destroy me?

Face pressed to her neck, I breathed in the scent of her skin, her arousal, her hair. I listened to her breathing, her heart racing. Every whimper sent lightning down my spine. She didn't remain still. No, she shifted her hips in time with the movement of my fingers, taking them deeper. Her skin bloomed with sweat; her head thrashed, her hair a wild tangle against the wall.

Her eyes were closed, her mouth pressed to my ear. "Fuck me, Darius. Fuck me now."

I lost control. That reserved voice and clipped tone. Begging. For me. To do exactly what I wanted more than I had ever wanted anything.

My wet fingers fumbled with the opening of my pants as I pulled my cock free and positioned myself. "Lily?"

"Yes," she breathed.

"I won't be able to control myself. I can't be gentle."

"I don't care."

The sound that came from my throat as I pressed into her, filled her, fucked her, made her mine was a mixture of pleasure and pain. I used both hands to hold her by her thighs, open and exposed and mine to take, just as the beast had done in her story.

Buried balls-deep, I pulled out slowly, then slammed deep.

Her panting turned into a keening wail as her core pulsed and spasmed around me, as she gave me the orgasm I'd demanded.

"Yes, yes! *Yes!*"

"That's it. Give yourself to me. Your control. Come, mate. Again. Fucking come again."

I moved hard and fast, fucking her until the only sound in the room was the slapping of skin on skin, until she surrendered to me. Again. And again. One orgasm rolled into another. Her entire body tightened like a bow, a scream erupting from her throat as she clenched and gripped my cock.

Seeing her pleasure was my undoing. My body shuddered, arched, the orgasm like a painful fist twisting my balls into a release that stole my breath and my sanity. I would never be the same. I knew and accepted the truth with an ease that would have shocked me mere hours ago.

I belonged to this woman. She was mine, and I would do anything—anything—to protect her.

Long minutes later my body cooled, and I tried to catch my breath, to be able to fucking see clearly. I still held her pressed to the wall, but she was soft and submissive in my hold, her hands stroking my hair now, no longer pulling.

This new, peaceful side of Lily filled me with contentment like I'd never known. I never wanted to move, wanted to remain buried inside her soft body for the rest of my life.

"Wow."

The word broke me from my trance, and I chuckled, male pride making me smile. "Did I do your beast justice?"

She turned her face away, her cheeks pink. Gently I kissed her jaw, her cheek, her face until she gave me her lips. When I had tasted her again and made my cock hard, I held her gaze and willed her to give me more truth.

"I want you again, Lily."

"You're still inside me."

I shifted my hips and she gasped. "Wall or bed?"

"I think I want to try the bed this time."

"Excellent choice." I carried her to the bed and settled her down so I could strip out of my clothing. Skin on skin. I needed to feel every inch of her, mark her, explore, touch, learn. Make her mine.

Tomorrow we would go on our first mission. Tomorrow we would be thrust back into the war.

Tonight she was mine.

3

*L*ily, *Moon Base Arturri, Mission Briefing Room*

EXHAUSTED WAS the right word for my state of being.

Sated.

Sore.

Happy.

Those were all brilliant words. As was *nervous*.

Nervous. There was a word. I was walking into a roomful of alien warriors from another planet who expected me to be one of them.

I was a librarian. A brilliant librarian, but still, I'd spent more time with books than with people. Any more than two or three people in a room was a rock concert as far as I was concerned.

So, of course there was standing room only in the briefing room, except for the two conspicuously empty seats in the front row. Which was just bloody brilliant if I wanted to be stared at, inspected and watched by every single person in the room.

Cue the drumroll please. Here is the freak from Earth. Oh, and if her hair is a mess, she's wearing no makeup, and she looks like she had no sleep because her new pair bond spent the entire night literally fucking every single functional brain cell out of her body? Please do the polite thing and pretend not to notice.

Meanwhile I would try like hell to pretend that did not accurately sum up my life for the last twenty-four hours.

"Welcome back, Darius." A tall, stunning redheaded female placed her hand on Darius's shoulder as he led the way around the front of the room so we could wind our way to our chairs.

"Thanks, Bantia. Ulixes." Darius inclined his chin to a tall, gorgeously dark male who stood next to her. They both wore Elite Starfighter uniforms exactly like the ones Darius and I were now wearing.

I heard Darius's name more than a dozen times as those gathered quietly welcomed him back into the fold.

But *welcome back?* As in, Darius was here before? Had he been a Titan?

Who was his partner? His pair-bonded mate? And where was she now?

Had he gotten tired of her and dumped her for me?

Was that a possible outcome for us as well? *Sorry, Lily, you don't meet my expectations. Moving on...*

The thought made me shudder, not with fear but with dread. Failing to meet expectations was one of my specialties. Just ask my mother.

Maybe his last pair bond was dead. Not saying that was a better outcome, but there was a small part of me that would rather just cease to exist than go through the humiliation of failing at being a Starfighter in real life. Failing Darius. Not being good enough. I'd had enough of that in my life, thank you very much.

Swallowing my nerves, I tried to focus on the here and now. This was an important meeting. All the Starfighter Titans were here. Two generals were here. I was an important person now. I had a job to do. A job that mattered.

Just like in the game, this was just my next mission with Darius. But this was even better. Real Darius. With real hands and real lips and those dark bedroom eyes making me feel like he was going to pounce and devour me.

I wanted more of that. And if I had to climb into a machine and go kick some ass to get more, that's what I would do. I had squeezed myself into the surprisingly flattering Elite Starfighter uniform with the silver swirl insignia on the chest. That design matched the dark swirl of the cipher implant site on my neck. And that matched Darius's mark, the Elite Starfighter mark everyone in the room seemed to carry.

According to what Darius had told me on the short walk to the meeting, there were Titan teams stationed on the Arturri moon base as well as General Jennix, commander of the Elite Starfighter mission control specialists. General Aryk and the Elite Starfighter pilots were reportedly running IPBM—Interplanetary Ballistic Missile—patrols as well as helping root out pockets of Dark Fleet resistance on the colony planet of Xenon.

Darius held out my seat and then settled beside me, glaring at anyone who looked like they were even thinking about talking to either one of us.

What was his problem? Was this supposed to be his version of acting protective? Because as far as I was concerned, he was being disrespectful and rude to everyone in the room but me. Flattering, in a dysfunctional way, but he appeared to have the manners of a randy goat. I could just hear my mother's scandalized gasp of disapproval all the way from Earth.

"What is your problem?" I whispered. "Stop glaring at everyone."

"There is no problem." Darius answered me, but his gaze continued to scan the room for something. Assassins? Someone he owed money? I had no idea what the hell was going on.

"Take your seats and quiet down." Bantia's voice carried well, and there was no doubting the respect shown her by everyone in the room. "General Romulus is waiting to give us a mission briefing from his location onboard the *Battleship Resolution*."

They dimmed the lights, and I leaned in closer to Darius so I could whisper in his ear. "And welcome back? What did she mean, welcome back?"

Darius stiffened next to me, and I caught the alert gaze of Ulixes watching us. "It's not important."

I was not a fool, but I did not want to make a scene. I crossed my arms over my chest and leaned back in my chair as the face of the Velerion General Romulus filled the screen. His voice was deep, his gaze direct. There were lines of exhaustion around his dark eyes and full lips. It was impossible to determine his age. He could have been anywhere between thirty and fifty years old. His face filled the once-blank space on the wall, and he appeared to be staring straight at me.

"Can he see us?" I asked Darius.

"Yes."

Brilliant. I should have packed some waterproof mascara and blush. With my pale skin I looked like a vanilla muffin that needed a bit more browning time in the oven. Half-baked and soft in the middle. Hell, soft everywhere. I was no warrior. I only played one in my video game.

"Welcome, Starfighters. I am pleased to introduce Titan Team Seven, Darius of Velerion, whom you should all remember, and his newly pair-bonded mate, Lily Wilson from Earth."

The room erupted into applause and shouts of excitement as we were formally introduced to the rest of the

Starfighters. When the brief round of cheers quieted, General Romulus continued.

"We welcome you both to the fight to defeat Queen Raya of Xandrax and her Dark Fleet allies."

With his next breath he launched into a fifteen-minute recap of their last mission where, apparently, Mia —*my friend Mia*—had saved the day like a real-life superhero. According to the general, bad guys had taken over a Velerion colony, enslaved the people, and forced them to use their factories to make a bunch of planet-destroying missiles, which had then been fired at both Velerion *and Earth.*

What the hell?

Why were they attacking Earth? We weren't part of this alien war.

Were we?

I breathed a sigh of relief when General Romulus shared that both missiles had been destroyed before reaching their destinations and that Elite Starfighter pilots continued to run around-the-clock patrols to intercept more.

Hence the reason I had yet to see Jamie. Assuming she was really here as Mia had claimed when she texted me.

The general displayed ship locations, planetary orbits that were identical to the fictional planets in the game. I had seen all of this before, in a headset back on Earth.

However, if I'd had any doubt that this was a real war, they were gone when he finished speaking. Either this was real, or I was in a coma somewhere back on Earth drooling on my straitjacket.

"Any questions?" Ulixes asked those assembled as he stepped forward. No one spoke.

"Good. Now, your mission, Titan Teams, is to infiltrate and destroy one of the few remaining underground facilities controlled by Queen Raya's forces on Xenon. We have cleared ninety percent of the planet's surface; however, we continue to encounter resistance. The facility we will destroy was built after occupation. The structure is heavily armored and has extensive ground defense weapons. We have our Starfighter MCS teams working on a jamming system that may blind the targeting computers; however, that will not prevent manual operation."

"How many?" Darius asked.

"Twenty aboveground turrets have been identified so far, but there may be more."

A few grunts were the only indication I had of whether twenty was an average number. During missions in the game—training simulation- I had to stop thinking of it as a game—during the *training simulations*, twenty would have been an above-average defense for one facility.

"Get your Titans ready, Starfighters. Shuttle pilots are on their way from Eos Station now to give you a ride. Mission specifics have been loaded into your Titans. I expect you all to be experts on that facility by the time you drop."

Bantia raised both hands above her head and yelled out, "Two hours, Titans."

Holy shit. I was going on my first mission in two hours? I hadn't even seen a Titan in real life yet. What if I didn't know how to work it? What if it was different?

"Ground and pound," someone spoke behind me.

All the Titans in the room lifted a fist and slammed it down on the table in front of them in a unified boom.

Just. Like. The. *Training. Simulation.*

The room cleared quickly as I stared at the now blank wall in front of us. For the first time since Darius had knocked on my door, this felt real.

Like I might die, I might get hurt...I might have to kill someone, real.

Darius watched me in silence until we were alone. He reached forward and touched my cheek with his fingers. "Are you all right?"

"I guess we'll find out."

He leaned in and kissed me until I melted.

"That's better." Forehead pressed to mine, he stared into my eyes. "Ready to climb into your Titan?"

4

*L*ily, Titan Tech Bay

SIX METERS TALL. Stealth black metal. The giant robot-looking Titan was armed with small missiles, loaded guns, and a host of other weapons buried beneath the Titan's outer shell. The word Athena and the Elite Starfighter emblem had been engraved over the chest plate.

"She's mine?"

Darius reached above his head and rested his bent arm on the giant Titan's leg. "Custom-made for you based on biometric scans acquired during training simulations." He patted the massive machine leg and looked up, way up, to the top of the Titan's body. "After we run this mission, you can request any necessary changes. We have our own tech team that will maintain and repair our Titans."

"We do?" This was all so much. Everything was larger than life. I felt like I was walking around on a psychedelic trip of some kind. "Where is yours?"

Darius grinned and pointed to a docking bay next to the one we were currently standing in. "Right next to you, where I belong."

I blushed. The heat crept up my cheeks, and there wasn't a damn thing I could do to stop it. I'd seen him naked. He'd seen me naked. I'd ridden his cock like a wild thing. So why was I blushing now? Damn it.

A loud voice filled the chamber. "Loading to commence. Titan One, clear your bay."

Bright green light flickered a warning, and a massive set of metal arms lowered from the ceiling to lift the Titan onto a track. I watched, fascinated, as it slid forward, then turned, heading for a loading area aboard a large shuttle of some kind.

The process looked exactly like I'd seen hundreds of times in the training simulation. Back on Earth, I'd admired the cut scenes and graphics, thought the artist's rendering of the inside of the base was pure sci-fi sweetness, the Titans fun to look at but not at all frightening.

Now?

The Titans were massive. Built for destruction. War. They were death machines. Chaos on the ground. The claw like fingers could puncture metal structures as thick as my arm was long. The targeting system inside could shoot down Scythe fighters or take out armed bunkers.

I stared at Darius's Titan as he walked to a tech display station and looked over the status report for his machine. "Looks good. Let's take a look at Athena, shall we?"

"Yes." Of course. In the training simulation, this had all happened automatically. But that had been a video game. This time I was going into battle firing real weapons.

Darius took my hand and led me to the display panel connected to my Titan as the overly loud announcements continued. They were loading Titan Eight.

"What numbers are we?" I asked.

"Thirteen and fourteen. We're team seven. We have a few minutes."

"Titan Team Seven. Right." I'd heard that fact during the briefing. Team Seven. Which meant there were six other teams, twelve other Titans that would be loaded before we would. But... "In the game—I mean training— it was first on, last off."

"Correct."

"And we're last on? First off?"

"Yes." Darius squeezed my hand even as he used his free hand to move over the control panel, his gaze glued to the Titan's status reports, not me. "Athena looks great. We're ready."

Ready? I'd been here less than a day, hadn't even been

inside my Titan, and we were going to be first out the door on Xenon, running straight into enemy fire?

Brilliant.

No, I was not okay. But I didn't really have a choice, did I? This was what I'd agreed to and, apparently, trained for. My heart pounded, and only half from fear.

In my real life, I was a wallflower. Introvert. Spent more time with books than humans. I was at the library so much I didn't dare have a pet, not even a cat. But in the game?

In the game I was brilliant. Fearless. Aggressive. I kicked everyone's ass, screamed at my enemies, and tore down walls with my bare hands. In the game, I was a monster.

And I had come to realize I enjoyed being that monster. I was tired of hiding all my emotions and acting as if everything was right with the world.

Sometimes a lady needed to scream out loud. And here was my chance.

Terrified? Yes. I was also excited. Adrenaline was flowing. I felt...alive.

Darius stepped back from the control panel as the announcer moved on to Titan Nine. "We'd better clear the bays." Still holding my hand, he tugged me along behind him. "Come. They'll have food and drink on the shuttle for us."

I walked beside him, and we fell in line with the other Elite Starfighter Titan teams boarding the passenger door of the large shuttle. The seats inside were comfortable but not fancy, and I buckled in next to Darius with my back to the shuttle wall. The space reminded me of the inside of military airplanes I'd seen in the movies where the soldiers sat in lines along the outside and the center was kept clear for ease of movement. The Titans were visible through a large window that separated the Starfighters from the back end of the transport shuttle, hung from long rails on the roof of the shuttle so they could roll out and launch more easily than if they were standing. And if the shuttle had to roll? Or was hit? They weren't going anywhere.

"Why Athena?" Darius's question made me blink.

"What?

"Why did you name your Titan Athena?"

"She's the Greek goddess of war."

Darius nodded as if that made perfect sense.

"And Tycho?" I asked. "Where did that name come from?"

He turned away from me. "It's a family name."

Okay. Apparently he didn't want to talk about it. Which was fine. For now. I had my own issues when it came to family, and I had no intention of discussing them in a shuttle full of Velerion Starfighters on their way to battle.

Two assistants came to each of us with food and drink offerings. I chose a bit of everything so I could taste it. There were both sweet and sour fruits. I preferred sweet. The meats reminded me of pepperoni and salami, and I assumed they were space food and were probably so processed and preserved they would outlive all of us. Didn't know if that was true or not, but I ate them on thick, dense bread that could have passed for naan back on Earth. The water was cold and crisp with a hint of something that reminded me of mineral water.

I was too nervous to eat much, but Darius helped himself to heaping loads of food, as did most of the others.

If I ate that much, it was coming back up. No question.

Hours may have passed—I wasn't sure—but as far as I was concerned, the trip was over too quickly. The sirens alerting us to move to the back and climb into our Titans made the hair on my arms stand at attention.

"You ready?"

"Ready." I unbuckled and followed Darius and the others through the sliding door that had opened into the Titan holding area. Ladders had dropped down from the railing system. I knew what to do. I'd seen this in the cut scenes of the video game as well.

Climbing onto the lowest rung, I held on as the railing system lifted me to the heart of the Titan. I stepped inside and took my place, my backside pressed to a cushioned support while my arms and legs slid within a suit that covered me from neck to toes like a second skin. The suit would read the nerve impulses as they traveled through my body. A twitch of my finger could fire a missile or shoot flames. Once activated, the heads-up display inside my Starfighter helmet would give me all the data I needed about my Titan. Location. System status. Weapons. Temperature. I could change direction with a flicker of my gaze on the map. Operating the Titan was as easy as breathing, the massive body felt like an extension of myself.

The canopy lowered to seal me inside, and I fought to keep my breathing slow and even. Next would be the chest plates and external shielding closing over the canopy. I would be blind to the outside world except for what I could see through my helmet display. The air I was breathing would be purified and recirculated, pressurized so I could fight in any environment, on any planet or in outer space. I was a walking spaceship; the jet packs attached to the Titan would allow me to fly short distances, if necessary. I couldn't go far, but I could go far enough to get away from an enemy...or follow one.

The comm system activated in my ear, and a now-familiar voice filled what I thought of as my vampire coffin. Like Dracula, I was alive in here. Sealed inside. Deadly. But still alive.

"Titan teams, this is General Romulus on *Battleship Resolution*. Mission details and coordinates have been programmed into your Titans, as well as known locations of ground defense systems. Deployment in ten minutes. You will have limited support from the air until you eliminate the ground defense systems. Good hunting."

The comm went dead, and my Titan fired up, every system going through the automatic launch sequence.

"Lily, can you hear me?" Darius's voice was calm, and I allowed the sound of his voice to sink into my bones.

"Yes. This is Lily. Go ahead."

"You're fourteen, Lily."

Fourteen? Right, Titan Fourteen. Last on. First off. Shit. I was going to be the very first one of us to hit the ground.

"Fucking brilliant."

"I'll be seconds behind you. Wait for me."

"Copy that." I was in no hurry to charge onto a foreign planet in a new machine I'd never operated.

Except that was a lie. Every single control, light, and sound was familiar. I knew the layout of this Titan better than I knew the car I drove every day to work at the library. The controls responded to my movements and commands exactly as they had in the ga— training simulation. This Titan might not be digital, but the display in my helmet was identical to the headset I wore on Earth. The hand controls, the system monitors. Heat. Weapon counts. Energy readings. Oxygen levels. Pressure sensors. The map. I recognized it all. I felt like I was trapped in the biggest déjà vu moment ever.

I was a six-meter-tall giant with a nearly indestructible exoskeleton, claws, and enough weaponry to blow up the entire city of London.

The rig jolted, and my entire body rumbled and shook as Athena, Titan Fourteen was rolled toward the launch doors. The rail system would catapult me in the direction I needed to go, and I would have to rely on my machine to hit the ground running.

"Here we go, Athena. Don't let me down."

"Of course not, Starfighter." The female voice was the one I'd chosen in the fighting simulation. The simple, recognizable voice calmed me more than anything else could have. "All systems are optimal. Launch in ten, nine, eight..."

The voice of the artificial intelligence that operated my Titan, aka Athena's voice, continued to count down as I settled into my seat and scanned all my readouts. This felt exactly like the game had. Same screens. Same joystick style controls and buttons. Same voice in my ear. "I can do this."

"I'm right behind you, Lily. Wait for me," Darius commanded.

When he'd said something similar in bed? Hot. My whole body had gone up in flames, and I'd come all over his cock, moaning his name as my fingernails dug into his back.

Now? Not so much. What the bloody hell did he think I was going to do? Hit the ground and run away from him? Hide? Battle everything on the planet by myself? Did he think I was suicidal or just stupid?

"...three, two, one, launch." Athena's voice confirmed what the heavy weight of my back against the Titan's cockpit already told me. I was launching forward with at least five or six G's of force shoving me into the seat and simultaneously trying to tear my cheeks off my face. I loved roller coasters, and this was one hell of a ride.

My screen filled with the planet's horizon as I hurtled toward the ground. The target was just ahead, the two outermost defense cannons almost in range as my Titan hit the ground with a thud and I kept running.

With a flicker of my gaze I silenced outgoing comms. I could still hear everything that was going on with the rest of the teams, but I had a tendency to talk to myself when I played—fought—whatever, and I didn't need Darius or any of the others listening to my babble.

"Athena, block outgoing comms unless I specifically address one of the other Titan's by name."

"Affirmative. Monitor and filter audio."

"Thanks."

"My pleasure, Starfighter Lily Wilson."

"Just call me Lily."

"Thank you for the honor. I shall address you as Lily."

"Brilliant."

"Of course, Lily. I am a Titan."

Was I arguing with a machine? Not arguing really, but why did I feel like this artificial intelligence was being elitist? Could a machine feel superior to other machines? How much did Athena really understand? Was she just an advanced computer, like we had on Earth? Or was she actually conscious? Alive?

"Lily, slow down!" Darius's command came through loud and clear. "You'll be in range of those cannons before I can reach you."

"No shit, Sherlock," I muttered. But what was Darius going to do about it? Pretty soon, we were all going to be target practice for Queen Raya's people.

"Sherlock is not a member of the Titan teams," Athena clarified.

"No, he's not."

"Then why did you address him? To whom shall I relay the message?"

This did *not* happen in the training simulation. "I was talking to myself."

Silence. Perfect.

As I approached the target zone, I analyzed the new data coming into my Titan. Three of the cannons had been moved to high ground since General Romulus had given us the mission briefing. Things had shifted, which meant the plan needed to change.

If we didn't take out the cannons mounted on the cliff walls, they would be shooting fish in a barrel.

"Athena, share the new cannon placement data with the rest of the Titan teams as well as mission command."

"Data transmitted."

"Good."

"Lily! Damn it, female. Wait for me. It's not safe."

"Really? I had no idea."

As if in direct response to my sarcasm, the nearest energy cannon fired a blast of blinding light in my direction. I jumped instinctively, Athena leaping over the blast like a deer clearing a fence. "Darius, I am heading for target bravo. It has been relocated into the canyon wall."

"I see that. Lily, don't go anywhere near there. I'll take care of it. It's too dangerous."

"Too dangerous for who?" I asked.

Athena answered. "Titan Tycho believes approaching target bravo is too great a threat to us, Lily."

"Why is that?"

I didn't expect an answer, but I got one anyway and wished I hadn't.

"Unknown. My calculations predict our success rate at seventeen percent higher than Titan Tycho's on his current trajectory."

Lordy. Now I had a talking calculator. What did Han Solo say? *"Never tell me the odds."*

A cannon blast lit up my screen. Heat soaked the right side of my body as my Titan's shields absorbed the hit. I had to dive and roll to evade a second attack. A third immediately followed, striking my Titan in the back and pushing me into a faster tumble. Damn it.

I skidded to a stop and hopped into a three-legged stance, weight on the balls of my feet, one hand down for balance, the other arm lifted, targeting systems locked on the nearest cannon.

I fired, the small missile screaming through the slight atmosphere until it exploded against the force field that surrounded the cannon.

Cursing, I fired again and shifted position as a neighboring cannon targeted and fired on my location.

"Lily! Get out of there!" Darius was practically screaming in my ear. I checked my maps. He was about fifteen seconds behind me, the next Titan right behind him and so on. Everyone was on the ground now. Running. Closing in.

"I'm fine." My proverbial hair was probably singed, but all my sensors indicated Athena was good to go. I'd taken a lot more damage than this in our training simulations. A *lot* more.

I ran for the cliffside, using boosters to increase my speed. When I was close enough, I leaped onto the side of the rock, the Athena's long claws extended from hands and feet. They pierced the soft, crumbling rock like diamond drill bits as I crawled up and up. And up.

Fifty meters. Eighty. A hundred meters. I could see the anchors that attached the base of the cannon to the rock above me, just out of reach.

I glanced below. The rest of the Titan teams had spread out and were attacking the previously mapped cannon positions. The two Titans assigned to the two additional cannons that had been unexpectedly relocated were making their own climbs.

And Darius in Tycho? He was climbing. Not fighting. Not helping the others. Not doing his bloody job.

Climbing. Behind *me*.

"Lily! Watch out!"

arius

A Scythe fighter appeared out of nowhere and dived toward Lily.

Queen Raya's fighters were small, fast, and nearly impossible to evade from the ground. I screamed a warning as the fighter fired on Lily's position.

"Lily! Watch out!"

My heart seized in my chest, the pain like pinchers tearing the organ in half. No air. I had no air. My vision blurred. Just like last time.

"Lily!" I willed myself up the cliff wall, using boosters to half crawl, half fly up the side to reach her. Nothing else mattered. Nothing.

Lily held on to the rock with one arm and swung her

entire Titan body wide as the Scythe fighter's blasters reached the rocks and exploded, sending debris raining down on my head.

A large rock hit me. I slipped. Lost my grip. Fell.

Caught hold.

I looked up. I was still too far away.

"Lily!"

"Darius, cool your jets. I'm fine." Her voice came through clipped and a bit loud. "What is your problem? This isn't half as hard as most of the missions in the training simulation. Leave me alone and go do your job."

Leave me alone? Go do your job?

Fuck. Now she sounded exactly like my big brother, Tycho, had before…

No. I wouldn't think about that. Nothing was going to happen to Lily. I was here. I would protect her, even from herself.

Firing my boosters on full, I let go of the cliff wall and flew up and over the cannon Lily had been climbing toward. Turning my boosters off to conserve fuel, I landed with a heavy thud on the ground just behind the turret.

The cannon rotated, the open-end square on my chest.

The cannon's energy built, the slight hum in the air alerting me to the imminent strike.

"Darius! What the hell are you doing?"

"Saving you."

Lily appeared on the opposite side of the cannon, her Titan body crawling up and over the edge of the slight ledge. I scowled despite the fact that she couldn't see my face.

"Get out of here. I'm about to destroy this thing, and the blast will burn through your armor."

"And your armor?" she asked.

"I'm not worried about me."

"You're an idiot."

"You're still here."

"I had this under control. What are you doing?"

"Go! Get out of here! Now!" I leaped up, firing my boosters, the cannon's targeting system following my every move, the length of the cannon rising as I did.

"Darius, you bloody idiot. You're not doing this."

Lily leaned forward, her Titan arms wrapping around the base of the cannon. With a loud screech that was half scream, half groan, she tunneled under the base and lifted.

"No!"

My protest fell on deaf ears as Lily lifted the entire cannon from the base. It was too heavy. I could have told her that.

The ground beneath her feet crumbled.

She shifted, sliding down and backward with a jolt of movement, the heavy cannon still in her arms as the ledge broke into pieces under the weight.

"I said, I've *got this*." Lily's voice was a roar in my head as she bent her knees and arched her back, flipping the heavy cannon onto her chest, then moving it to her head. Then over.

She fell as the cannon fell, just a few meters behind as they both raced to sure destruction on the ground below.

"Lily!" I saw the future. Broken bones. Blood. Lifeless eyes.

I couldn't do it. Not again.

The cannon hit the ground and exploded in a ball of flame that engulfed my pair-bonded mate completely. I saw nothing but fire.

Without fuel to burn, the flame flickered and died within seconds. I searched the ground, used the last of my booster fuel to fly down to the ground and find her. My mate. My pair-bonded mate. My life. My future. My everything.

I landed to find her in a crouch, waiting for me. She was unharmed, her Titan in perfect condition. She had flipped, used her boosters and landed in a crouch with perfect, Elite Starfighter timing.

"Lily? Are you all right?"

"Do. Not. Speak. To. Me."

That was the last thing she said before rising to her full height. Standing toe to toe, we were of equal size. Equal strength. Our Titans identical except for the names etched in the exoskeletal armor and the warrior controlling them.

"Lily?"

Turning on her heel, the Titan Athena and her warrior driver ran into the battle raging behind me. I followed. I would always follow.

———

Lily

How dare he?

How dare he?

If I weren't using my giant metal fists to punch the rocky base of the last cannon into dust—Darius's cannon, the one he'd been assigned to take out, the one he'd ignored to chase after me like I was a helpless child—I would be beating the hell out of that man instead.

Had I been nervous to drop onto an alien world? Yes. First out of the gate? Bigger yes. But the moment my Athena's feet hit the ground, something had happened.

I'd become the badass fighter in the game again. I wasn't Lily the Librarian; I was Elite Starfighter Lily in Athena, her Titan goddess of war, and I was ready to kick some *ass*.

"Lily? Are you well?"

Of course he had followed me.

His Titan's fist landed near mine, and the stone base the ground cannon was mounted to crumbled on one side.

Darius reached back to punch it again, but I shoved him out of the way.

"What are you doing?" he yelled.

"What am I doing?" I yelled back, so furious I could feel my pulse pounding in my temples. I had a raging headache, and I tasted blood in my mouth from biting my cheek. "What am I doing?"

Back home, I didn't have a temper. Such a display was unladylike. My mother had made sure I knew how to control myself, hide what I was feeling, from a very young age.

Somehow, being in this Titan fighter on another planet ripped every emotional Band-Aid from my modest, quiet, mouselike heart and turned me into a beast.

Yes, that's what I felt like, an Atlan beast, filled with fighting rage. Huge. Powerful. Unstoppable.

Jumping up onto the top of the cannon, I wrapped my Titan arms around the firing tube, braced my feet against the base, and pulled. Twisted. Hard.

The cannon's metal screeched with a fingernails-on-chalkboard rending sound as the firing bit tore away from the base.

"What. Am. I. Doing?" I whispered the question, and Darius backed up a few paces to look at me, his hands out in front of him as if warding off an attack.

Oh, he was going to get an attack, all right.

"Analysis of your tone indicates you are angry. I have been allowing your communications to Elite Starfighter Darius to broadcast on your private comm frequency."

"Good." I wanted him to know I was furious with him and his lack of faith in me. His overprotective bullshit.

Lifting the cannon piece, I threw it in his direction,

not to hit him, but as a message. He avoided the large chunk easily. "Lily, talk to me. What is wrong?"

"What's wrong?" Was he actually asking me that? And why was I suddenly on the verge of tears? Fucking brilliant.

The other Titan teams took down the last of the ground assault cannons, and I looked up as alarms blared in my helmet. Scythe fighters incoming. Lots of them.

"Move, Titans!" General Romulus's voice jolted me from my own thoughts and back into action.

I jumped down from the rock and ran toward the entrance to Queen Raya's bunker. More weapons fired from vents in the heavy doors, but they were much smaller than the cannons we'd just wiped out like a swarm of killer bees. They would pose no real danger. It was the fighters coming in from above that could destroy one of us.

"Lily! Take cover!"

"No!" I ran for the door, rage fueling me as hot blood poured through every cell in my body. I was not a child to be coddled and protected. I was not some silly girl who didn't know how to protect herself, how to fight. I was an Elite Starfighter, and Darius had damn well better learn that and accept it, or we were going to have serious problems.

Maybe we already did.

I fell in step next to Bantia and Ulixes, the three of us the front line of an assault formation that spread out behind us like wings. We were the tip of the spear.

My blood pounded. Adrenaline flooded my already exhausted system. But we weren't finished yet.

"Scythe fighters! Coming over the ridge!" someone shouted. I didn't recognize the voice, but Athena's displays informed me it came from someone in Titan team four.

Looking up as I ran, I saw two fighters blast over the top of the cliffs I'd just been climbing, moving faster than any jet I'd ever seen. Two more. Four. They were all in battle formations that I recognized from *Starfighter Training Academy.*

"Lily! Wait for me!"

"Four in the rear, take a knee and shoot those Scythe fighters out of the sky," General Romulus ordered.

Display data showed the last four Titans peel off and take positions to defend the rest of us. Darius was one of them. I could hear him cursing in my helmet.

"Fuck! Goddamn it! Lily!"

But he did as General Romulus ordered.

"Break down that door. Ground assault is two minutes out." Bantia's order was clear and precise. We had two minutes until the smaller assault teams would be pouring into this bunker like water. Assuming we had the door open for them.

"On it!" I shouted, then used my boosters to fly to the topmost opening in the door. A large energy weapon rotated toward my face. I wrapped one Titan hand around the tip and pulled with all the power I could get from Athena.

The weapon hummed; the power surge so strong I could feel it pulsing up my arm inside the Titan's protective armor.

Athena's voice filled my helmet. "Lily, recommend you disengage. The weapon will destroy us in six... five...four..."

With a scream of frustration, I put every ounce of rage and fear and anxiety I'd felt since leaving Earth into my next pull.

The weapon broke free with a loud *pop*, and I tossed it to the ground over my shoulder.

"Nice one, rookie," Bantia said. She was below me and to my left, tackling the next weapon.

"Thanks." At least someone appreciated my skills.

Using my claws, I dug into the wall and used the weight of my Titan to slice my way down to the next opening. This one was actively firing, so I lowered my arm to the corner and shot a grenade inside.

Three seconds later, the weapon exploded, mid-fire, the blast twice the size it would have been otherwise. The wreckage exposed an additional section of the bunker wall, blasting off the thick metallic shielding to reveal a series of weight-bearing structures that reminded me of trusses beneath a roof. Except thick. Heavy. Indestructible. Layers deep, like a maze.

We were never getting through this wall with a frontal assault. We'd have to blow the entire side of the cliff to even make a dent.

Looking behind me, I watched Darius shoot down a

Scythe fighter, the small ship spiraling out of control as it dived into the ground and burst into flames.

On the other side of the battle area another fighter had already crashed and burned to a crisp. I winced.

No one could have survived that.

So far I'd taken out unmanned guns, not people. But that could change at any moment.

"Let's go, Lily! Let's finish this." Bantia's Titan leaped into the opening I'd created and disappeared inside the maze. Ulixes was right behind her as I hung onto the side of the wall with one clawed hand and two feet still puncturing the shielding material.

"We have to open it from the inside," Ulixes said, then disappeared behind his pair-bonded fighting partner.

I looked back over my shoulder to make sure Darius was alive and well. He was. Cursing and firing like a battle-crazed berserker. Running toward my position.

"Lily!"

Ignoring his shout, I dropped down to the opening to follow Bantia and Ulixes inside. Within seconds complete and total darkness swallowed me whole.

6

NOTHING LIKE WALKING on beams in total pitch-black. Athena's infrared and sonar systems were providing me with a visual display, but it wasn't clear.

"Athena, can't you clean that up? I can't see."

"Negative, there is too much interference from their jamming frequencies."

"Brilliant." I took two more steps. The Titan's left foot slipped, and I barely caught the massive body with my right hand. "This is ridiculous. Give me a flashlight and open the shielding so I can see with my own eyes."

"Defensive shielding will be at fifty percent."

"I don't care. I need to see."

"Understood." With a few loud clicks and swooshing noises, the front shielding that covered my face slid away so that I was protected only by my helmet and the translucent canopy. Bright floodlights pierced the darkness for three to four meters in front of me, and I sighed with relief. It wasn't perfect, but at least I could see where I was going.

"Lily, I've lost sight of you. Report." Bantia's voice gave the order.

"Line-of-sight visibility is three to four meters. Only way to see is without full shielding. Using only canopy and helmet cover."

"Ulixes?" she asked.

"I can't see a fucking thing. The jammers are getting stronger the deeper we go."

"Go to visual. And be careful."

"Copy that," Ulixes said.

The other two Titan's lights turned on, and between the three of us, I could just make out enough of the structure to see a spiral pattern. "Up or down?"

Light appeared behind me. I turned to find Darius in Tycho just a few steps away. "Both. Bantia and Ulixes go down; Lily and I will head up."

"Aren't you supposed to be out there shooting down Scythe fighters?" I asked.

"Air support from the Elite Starfighter pilots came in and wiped them out. They are patrolling the airspace. We're clear."

I looked at the set of lights I assumed belonged to

Bantia. "We could head back out and tell the pilots to blow this door into pieces."

"Negative. It's too thick. We'd need battleship cannons to get through," Ulixes said.

"And there would be nothing left," Bantia added.

I didn't think we cared much if there was anything left of the place, but then I had no idea how many people were inside. What if they had children here? "All right."

Bantia leaped down three levels and caught a beam with her Titan hands, swinging to drop down on the level below. Ulixes cursed.

"Damn it, female."

She laughed. "Keep up then."

The two took off like bouncing fireflies in the darkness. I looked at Darius, then up. And up. We were about equidistant from both top and bottom. Jumping down suddenly seemed a lot easier than climbing. "Let's go."

Using my boosters for an assist, I leaped up and landed on the beam above me.

"Careful," Darius instructed.

"You didn't tell Bantia or Ulixes to be careful," I pointed out, jumping to the next beam.

"I'm not in love with them."

Shit. I nearly missed the beam, caught myself with the claws on my right foot as my right hand missed the handhold entirely.

Darius jumped up to the beam I had just abandoned.

Love? He loves me? After one day? And he tells me

now? Not when he was buried inside me. Not when I was gasping and clawing at him, screaming his name. Now?

And love? Like real, honest-to-goodness love? How was that possible? My parents had known me their entire lives and barely remembered to send me a card at Christmas.

Leaping again, I overshot the mark and grappled for a hold on the beam above where I'd been aiming. Thank goodness the Titan's arms were a lot stronger than mine. I pulled myself up and took a couple of slow, deep breaths. I could do this. I was not rattled and on edge simply because the sexiest man I'd ever met had treated me like a helpless child one moment, then told me he was in love with me the next.

Was this tightness in my chest anger? Anxiety? Frustration? Disbelief? Pain? I didn't know, and trying to figure it out was making me shaky and distracted. I wanted Darius to love me, badly. I simply couldn't accept the fact that the emotion came so easily to him.

Not even my own mother loved me. I was tolerated. A tool to make her look like a good parent. Sent to the best schools, the best universities. The best clubs. The best of everything. And not once had she attended a recital or award ceremony. No matter how hard I tried, she never cared. I finally figured out the problem; I was the textbook definition of *unlovable*.

Athena's feet safely planted on the beam, I looked down. And down. I could see nothing in the darkness, not even Bantia's and Ulixes's lights. I felt like I was standing over an abyss that wanted to swallow me whole.

"Lily? Are you all right?"

"I'm fine. Try to keep up."

Darius chuckled and I felt the tightness around my heart loosen a little. "Vega help us, you sound like Bantia already."

The idea of being as strong, confident, and skilled as Bantia seemed to be, pleased me.

Moving quickly, I reached the top level of the structure, Darius arriving less than a minute behind me.

"What now?" I asked, looking around at...nothing. Stone. Beams. There was nothing here that looked like any kind of control, wiring or power source. Just rocks and darkness.

Darius stood next to me in his Titan, and we used our combined light to widen the viewable area. Still, I saw nothing.

"Team One? You see anything? We are at the top, and there is nothing here."

"Stand by." Ulixes voice sounded gruff and like he was nearly out of breath.

A loud boom sounded from below, and the structure we were standing on vibrated under our feet, then shook, shifting enough that I had to use my Titan claws to hold my position.

"We're in," Bantia said. Then I heard nothing but static. Both Ulixes's and Bantia's locator beacons disappeared from my sensors.

"Athena? Where is Team One?"

"Unknown. We lost the signal when they entered the compound."

"Shit." I glanced down. Way down. "Should we go after them?"

Darius was silent for a few seconds. The beams shifted beneath us again. "We need to get out of here. The whole thing is going to collapse."

As if the beams were listening to him, a loud series of popping noises sounded from below.

Darius turned to the outer wall and fired a grenade that looked like a cannonball with claws. The sharp arms penetrated the wall several meters below us and stuck like Velcro.

"Take cover!" Darius yelled at me. I turned away from the blast, but there really wasn't anywhere to go.

Darius's Titan draped itself over my Titan's back as the explosion ripped through the enclosed space. "Shielding up, Lily. Full body armor. Now."

I wasn't about to argue. Apparently Athena's artificial intelligence had also decided that was the best course of action, because my canopy was now fully enclosed with Titan armor once more and I was blind except for my sensors.

The beams shuddered, collapsed about a meter, and clumped to a stop at an odd angle. The structure was not going to be standing for long.

"Turn around. We're going to leap to the shielding

wall, slide down with our claws and climb out the hole we just made. Understood?"

I sighed. He was right and I knew it. There was no sense arguing with him. I wanted to go after Bantia and Ulixes, but we could do that more easily from the ground. Blow a new hole in the base and get in there...now that we knew what this damn thing was made of.

I turned to face the back side of the shield doors and leaped forward, catching myself with extended claws that penetrated the metal. With a few adjustments and finger flexing I was sliding down the wall at a nice, smooth pace, my claws cutting through the heavy metal like butter.

If it hadn't been so dark, I would have felt like a pirate with a knife, riding down the center of a sail. Except maybe I needed a white pirate blouse, tight black leather pants, a nice, tight bustier, and a parrot on my shoulder. Now *that* would be an adventure.

Darius could be the sexy young stud about to walk the plank, waiting for me to swoop in and save him.

Like that would ever happen. He'd probably dive in the water, wrestle a few sharks, and take over the entire ship.

Maybe then he'd fuck me up against the mast of the ship during a storm. Lightning strikes illuminating the sky. Sea spray landing on his back. A canopy of stars over our heads. The two of us alone and unafraid, ready to cash in all the pirates' treasure and retire to a tropical island where we would have sex in a hammock, or on the beach—sand be damned—or with me bent over a barstool, buzzed on piña coladas as he filled me from behind.

The bright light coming through the opening Darius's grenade created was like a flash bomb inside my helmet. Athena adjusted at once, but I was still blinking hard and trying to regain my bearings as I swung my feet out through the opening, then rolled so my Titan's chest faced the outside of the blast door. I dug my claws back in so I could slide the rest of the way down.

"Status, Athena?" I asked.

"No hostile forces within range."

Nice. At least I didn't have to worry about being shot off the wall like a sitting duck. I could have used my boosters to basically fly down, but why waste the energy. I might need them later. Because until we were inside this place, this mission was not over.

Glancing up, I watched as Darius performed an identical maneuver to mine, swinging through the opening, flipping, grabbing onto the exterior with his claws. He was sliding down the wall with me, keeping pace until our Titans' feet touched solid ground.

"Athena, can we blast a hole here without endangering the others?" I asked.

"Unknown."

Damn it. I wanted to get in there, but I didn't want to hurt Bantia or Ulixes if they were directly on the other side of the blast.

Facing the giant door, I turned to my right to count off twenty paces. On the inside, Team One had taken off to my left. Assuming they continued that direction, this should be safe.

"Where are you going?" Darius asked.

"Keep up." At my mark, I backed away from the door, lifted my arm, and fired my largest grenade at the door, chest high. I wanted the largest hole possible, and losing half of my blast radius in the rock under the door would be a waste. "Fire in the hole!" I yelled.

Darius's Titan tackled me to the ground as a giant plume of rock and debris rained down on us from the blast.

"What are you doing?" I yelled.

"Are you insane?" Darius's voice sounded off. Shaky. "You should have let me do that."

"Why? Because I'm a girl?"

He growled, the sound one of frustration. "Because you're mine."

Two nearby Titan teams ran for our location, then disappeared inside the entrance I'd created. Brilliant. I made the opening, and they beat me inside. "Get off me."

"You weren't saying that last night."

Oh God, I was going to kill him with my bare hands.

"Get. Off."

"No. We've done our job. Ground forces are already on the move."

I turned my Titan-sized head to see that he spoke the truth. Hundreds of smaller attack units were racing toward us, armed to the teeth, battle cries on their lips. They wore armor exactly like I'd seen when I was playing what I'd once believed was only a video game. The stats on the armor were impressive, and I knew they could take a hit. More than one.

As if on cue, the general's voice resonated inside my helmet.

"Stand down, Titans. Guard the perimeter. Ground forces are now engaged." As General Romulus gave a direct order, I didn't dare disobey it. Not on my first mission as a Titan.

Not when I was so angry with my perfect, sexy, pair-bonded *mate* that I was seeing red.

One minute I wanted to jump him, the next? Scream at him. And after that? Shit. I just wanted to cry. I was an emotional roller coaster, and I hated every second of it.

Why didn't Darius trust me to take care of myself? Why did everyone in my life have to treat me like I didn't know what the hell I was doing? Like a walking mistake? A clutz? An idiot who needed careful advice and tending? I was tired of being treated like a wallflower.

Was this what love was supposed to be? Passion? Caring? Was this putting another's needs before one's own? I didn't think so, but then, I'd never been in love before, so I had no idea how I was supposed to feel.

Did Darius really love me? After so short a time together? He was an alien, but he was still a man. Most of the men I knew on Earth, including my own father, weren't big on monogamy or commitment in general. Why would an alien be any different?

"You can get off me, Darius. I'm not going to run away."

Slowly, as if afraid he might startle a scared rabbit, Darius moved his Titan off mine and held out a massive hand to help me to my feet. I took it, not because I couldn't get up on my own, but because I was too tired to fight with him. The adrenaline that had powered through my body was gone, leaving me to crash and burn to cinders inside my own mind. I didn't understand any of this, and I hated the fact that I felt so unsure.. Hated that I wasn't confident of my place in this group of Titans or with Darius. I'd thought I was sure about him, and then he'd been welcomed back, already a Titan. He was keeping secrets from me. Big secrets.

I knew the secrets game, had played that game my whole life, and I hated it.

I hated that Darius was hovering over me like a helicopter parent making sure I felt like I couldn't do anything on my own. Acting like I should be scared when I wasn't.

This was more real than anything I'd ever done before. Should I be frightened? Because as soon as I'd slipped inside Athena's huge, powerful frame I'd felt powerful. Strong. Nervous but excited, too. Was that wrong? Was that how Mia and Jamie had felt on their first missions? Sure, I wasn't excited about the prospect of killing a living being, but I hadn't been terrified of dying either.

Perhaps I should have been.

Or perhaps I should be more worried about giving my heart to an alien who had no intention of responding in kind.

"Team Seven, cover the entrance. I don't want any surprises down there."

"Yes, General." Darius moved to stand on one side of the blast area, and I stood with my back to the blast door on the other.

We stood in silence, scanning the terrain for enemy Scythe fighters, random enemy attacks. Nothing.

Then a rumble deep in the ground.

"What was that?" I asked.

"I don't know." Darius and I crouched in a defensive posture, weapons ready. "General, there is a ground disturbance."

"Copy that. *Resolution's* sensors are picking it up. Hold your position."

"Holding position."

I didn't say a word, but I had a bad feeling. A really bad feeling.

The rumbling increased until the ground shook like an earthquake.

A moment later Bantia burst through the wall, ground troops running at full speed behind her. She stood at the opening, urging the smaller forces to greater speed.

"Move! Move! Move!"

"What's happening?" I asked.

"It's a trap. The whole fucking thing is empty. But

there's enough explosive down there to make a crater out of the whole area. Get out of here!"

Reaching behind me, I buried my claws in the metal wall and pulled, peeling the opening wider bit by bit, relieved when I saw there was enough room for even one more soldier to squeeze through. "More!" I yelled.

Darius followed suit as Bantia joined me in peeling back the shielding. We weren't doing much, but if we saved even a handful of lives, it would be worth it.

"Where's Ulixes?" Darius asked.

Bantia answered between grunts as we tugged together. "Bringing up the rear, of course. As usual." There was frustration and worry in her tone, but admiration as well. Trust that he would be all right. And I missed those touches in Darius's prior rantings at me all the more.

"How long do we have?" I asked.

"I don't know. Not long."

Shuttles were doing touch-and-goes on the ground near us, hovering just low enough for the evacuating troops to leap onboard. The moment they were full, they soared away, another waiting to take its place.

I lost count of the troops as they poured out of the wall, running at full speed. Finally Ulixes appeared.

"Clear."

"Thank Vega," Bantia said. "Let's get out of here."

Turning together, we all ran for the nearest shuttle large enough to hold our Titan frames. Darius paced behind me, but I wasn't going to waste energy yelling at him to hurry. My bad feeling had gone from mild anxiety to full-blown panic attack. We had to get out of here.

Now.

The first blast knocked me to my knees. The shock wave lifted my Titan and threw me into the cliff wall more than twenty meters away.

I slid down to slump on the rocky ground. I hurt, but everything seemed to be intact.

I looked up and winced, threw my arms up to protect my Titan's chest as chunks of rock and twisted metal fell from the sky to bury me alive.

arius, Battleship Resolution, Medical Station

"WHERE IS SHE? Let me see her. Now." Lily. My pair bond was hurt, and she was here. Somewhere.

"She's in surgery, sir. You need to calm down and have a seat." The placating, soothing voice of the medical officer had the opposite effect. I wasn't calm. I couldn't do this. Not again.

"Give me a fucking sterile suit. I don't care what I have to do. I have to get in there."

The large male officer frowned, clearly out of patience. "You need medical attention yourself, Starfighter. You are covered in sweat and dust, you have blood on your face, and you will do nothing but scare the medical team. So get your ass in that room." He pointed to a medical treatment room a few paces away marked with the number four. "Get on the exam table and shut the fuck up before I call security."

Well, this was a battleship, not a civilian hospital. And this medical officer was no low-ranking idiot but a captain. Probably a fully trained physician as well as a soldier. He wasn't going to budge.

The faster I got my own wounds taken care of, the sooner I could get to Lily.

I walked into the exam room, and the door slid closed behind us, the reflective surface activating to give us privacy as he ran a medical scan.

"Two broken ribs. Second-degree burns on the neck and left hand. A bit of bruising. You'll be fine." He gave me the reassurance even as he held a treatment injector to the burned area on the side of my neck. With a quick movement of his hand, the injection activated. The medication flowed into my flesh. It burned like acid, but I didn't say a word.

"This should take care of any residual bruising as well as speed healing of the burns. I am going to recommend you remain off duty for the next two days."

"Are we done here?" Lily. I had to get to Lily.

"Not quite." A second injection followed, this time over my broken ribs. The ache I'd been feeling for the last hour faded at once but was quickly replaced with sharp, stabbing agony that lasted several minutes. When it was over, he held the scanner over my ribs again. "Excellent. Your bones are healthy. The breaks have healed."

"Great." My forehead was covered in sweat. I'd had my bones patched before, but that didn't make it hurt less.

"Yes. I'm prepared to release you from my care. However, you will not be allowed anywhere near your pair bond in your current condition."

"What condition?"

"You're filthy. Clean yourself up, Starfighter. I don't care how in love with you she is; even she won't want to touch you until you take a shower."

I stood and walked to see my reflection in the large sliding door. The sight that greeted me was not pleasant. My hair was spiked and grimy. My skin was streaked with paler lines where sweat had created a map through the dust on my face. I probably smelled as bad as I looked.

Damn Vega and every other star. He was right. I could not go to Lily like this.

Waving my hand in front of the door's release scanner, I waited impatiently, shoving through before it had opened even halfway.

"You're welcome!" The medical officer's voice followed me down the corridor, but he was laughing. In fact, I would probably be the laughingstock of the entire battleship in the next few hours. Nothing men liked better than to give one another a hard time for falling in love.

And I wasn't just in love. I was obsessed. Possessive. Protective. I wanted to lock Lily in our bedroom and never let her out. Keep her naked and sated and safe.

If she'd allow me. Which, based on her reactions during this last mission, was going to be a tough sell. Even if I couldn't keep a fellow Starfighter out of battle, I could protect her. Move in first in the most dangerous situations. Do everything possible to keep her out of the line of fire.

Whether she liked it or not.

I was not going to lose another person I loved on the battlefield. Never again. And if that made Lily angry, then so be it. I could deal with my woman's anger. In fact, I would keep her so well pleasured, so in love with me that she would accept my faults, my need to keep her safe. Every time she raged, I would soothe her with pleasure.

Starting now.

———

Lily, Medical Station, Surgical Recovery

THE ANESTHESIA WORE off as if someone had snapped their fingers. One second I was unconscious, the next I was wide awake in a hospital bed of some kind. Taking stock of my situation, I moved bit by bit, testing things out. My leg was sore, and I had a slight headache, but that seemed to be the worst of it.

I sat up, ready to find out what the hell had happened to me.

I remembered being buried in Athena, tons of rock

piling on top of my Titan, every alarm and sensor blaring at me that we were in trouble. The sound of Darius yelling my name. Long minutes of darkness when I was completely alone.

And pain. Mindless, staggering pain.

In my leg.

Lifting the sheet covering me, I looked at the leg in question and frowned. There was a transparent bandage covering half of my thigh. No stitches. No blood. Just a weirdly large, sticky bandage that I could see my skin through. It looked fine. Maybe I'd been dreaming.

I wiggled my toes. Flexed my foot. Bent my knee. Tried to lift my leg.

"Damn it!" *That* hurt.

"Don't move yet. The bone isn't completely healed and won't be for several more hours." A doctor or nurse or medic, I had no idea which, walked around the foot of my bed with a scanner of some kind, reading data I couldn't see.

"Hours?"

She looked up, and I was struck by the brightness of her pale gray eyes. "Yes, the femur is a very large bone in human anatomy, and yours was snapped in three places."

"Three places?" I felt like a fool repeating everything she said, but I was trying to figure out how a broken bone could heal in just a few hours.

"Yes. Are you in pain?"

I thought for a moment. "Only when I try to move it."

"Excellent. That will improve as the bone continues to

mend. By tomorrow morning you should be fully healed."

"How is that possible?"

"We surgically implanted osteobots along the breaks. They will rebuild your bone." She patted me on the ankle. "Don't worry, the diaphysis will actually be stronger than it was before."

"The what?"

"The long part of your bone. In the middle."

Was she *trying* to make me feel stupid?

"Normally we would simply do an injection, but your bone fragments required realignment as well."

Fragments? Gross. I suddenly could picture a surgeon with a knife and a pair of pliers trying to move pieces of my femur around. Not cool. This conversation was making me sick.

Don't ask.

Don't you bloody ask...

"Where's Darius?"

Damn it. Idiot. He wasn't here. That was where he was. Somewhere else. Maybe he was hurt.

"He was creating a disturbance after his treatment. I do not know where he is now."

"A disturbance? What kind of treatment? Is he hurt?"

She sighed, but the sound was more tired than anything else, so I let it go.

"Let's see. Elite Starfighter Darius. Ah yes, here he is." She scrolled through the data as I would have scrolled through a social media feed on my phone, pausing to scan, then moving her fingers again. "Two broken ribs. Bruises. A few minor burns. He was treated and released. He's going to be fine."

Relief flooded me and I tried to hold on to my anger from before, during the mission, but it drained out of me like someone had pulled the plug on a tubful of bathwater. Gone.

"How do I find him?"

She grinned. "I'll put out a shipwide call. In the meantime"—her smile was infectious—"you have other visitors. If you feel up to it?"

"Who?"

The door slid open, and two people I had once believed I would never, ever meet came into the room like they owned the place. "Lily!"

The nurse left the room as I looked them over, a huge smile breaking on my face. I knew them well, from the unmistakable Starfighter uniforms to the faces I'd grown to care about back on Earth. "Jamie? Mia? Oh my God, what are you doing here? How did you even know I was here?"

"Oh shit, your accent is even cuter in person." Jamie clapped her hands and came around to my left side. "I have got to learn how to talk British."

"I'm stationed here. I followed your mission at MCS." Mia rolled her eyes at Jamie, her thick German accent making me smile even more than Jamie's exuberant American one. "Jamie has been driving me absolutely insane. Since we knew you were coming, every single moment she's been talking about the three of us meeting."

"No, not meeting, going out clubbing. Dancing. We need to get drunk and dance and drive our men crazy."

Mia chuckled. "A tight black dress and a rave would certainly make Kass lose his mind a bit."

Jamie was smiling. "Oh yeah. Alex wouldn't last an hour. He'd throw me over his shoulder and have his way with me in a bathroom stall."

I nearly choked on my own spit. "What?"

Jamie sat down on the side of my bed and took my hand. "Don't tell me Darius isn't smoking hot and totally in love with you?"

"He's definitely smoking hot."

Mia, brilliant, annoying Mia caught on to what I didn't say. "But he's not in love with you? How is that possible?"

"I don't know. But he's not."

"Have you, you know, had sex?" Jamie asked.

"Yes."

"Was it good sex?" Mia asked.

I had to be three shades of red by now. Proper ladies did *not* discuss this kind of thing. "I think so."

"You think so?" Jamie, so forward. Blunt. She was exactly the way I'd always imagined Americans to be. I simultaneously judged her for it and wished I wasn't so reserved. I had my maniacally controlling mother to thank for that.

Mia watched me, her gaze more intense than I was prepared to defend against. "You were a virgin."

"Mia!" Brilliant. Did I have the word *virgin* written across my forehead in red ink?

Jamie leaned back with a gasp but didn't let go of my hand. "Oh dear. Well, did he take care of you? Was it good? Did you enjoy yourself?"

"Did you come?" Mia asked. "Have an orgasm?"

Now who was the blunt one?

"Or two?" Jamie added.

"Yes. It was good. Sex isn't the problem."

Jamie wiggled her hips to sit even closer. "Spill."

Mia glanced over her shoulder toward the closed door. "Are those things soundproof?"

She looked from Jamie, who shrugged, to me.

"I have no idea," I said.

"Well, let's keep our voices down, shall we? Our men are right outside."

"What?" I hissed, not a bit happy to hear this news. We were discussing my sex life with two alien men I didn't know standing right outside the door?

Mia leaned close, as did Jamie, until I felt like we were in a footballers' huddle, foreheads nearly touching. "So, what is going on with you and Darius?"

"And how can we help?" Jamie asked.

I squeezed both of their hands. "You already have. It's so wonderful to meet you both in person. I can't believe we are on another planet."

"Yeah, and back home everyone still thinks *Starfighter Training Academy* is just a game."

"How many people do you suppose are playing right now?" Mia mused. "Right this very moment?"

"Tens of thousands," I guessed.

Jamie sighed. "Well, I wish they would hurry up and beat the game. We need them. This war is not going well, in case you didn't notice." She glanced down at my bandaged leg, still uncovered from when I'd moved the sheet. "What am I talking about? Of course you noticed."

The war wasn't going well? What did that mean?

"Forget about the war," Mia insisted. "Tell us about Darius. What's the problem?"

"I don't know. The sex was great. Then we went to our first mission briefing, and I found out he was already a Titan...with a different partner."

"Who?" Jamie asked. "A woman? Is he pair bonded to someone else?"

"Did she die?"

"I don't know. He hasn't said a word about it, and I haven't had time to ask."

Jamie winced in empathy. "Well, if she died, I could see how he wouldn't want to talk about it. Might be too painful."

Exactly. "Which is why I don't think he's in love with me. The sex is good, but there's something missing, you know? He doesn't talk to me. He's not honest. He's keeping secrets. And worse than that..."

I stalled, but Mia was having none of it. "Worse than that is what?"

"He was completely psycho on our last mission. Shoving me out of the way, ordering me to wait for him instead of doing my job. He treated me like I had no skill and no idea what I was doing."

"You're an Elite Starfighter. Damn right you know what you're doing." Jamie jumped to my defense.

Mia, however, had grown pensive. "Maybe you should give him a chance. If he lost his pair bonded in battle, maybe he's afraid it will happen again. Maybe he's afraid to lose you, too."

"Maybe." The idea was worth considering, but even that wouldn't excuse not telling me about his past. I'd felt like an idiot in that briefing room, everyone there knowing his history but me. Me! When I was supposed to be the one he loved, his pair bonded, the one he shared everything with and trusted above all others. His freaking wife, for goodness' sake. Or as close to a marriage as these Velerions got.

The nurse came back into the room with a smile pasted on her lips, the same smile I'd seen on nurses' faces back on Earth. The I'm-here-and-it's-time-for-every-one-else-to-leave smile. "Let's get you cleaned up, Lily."

I glanced down at my hands, clasped on either side by my friends, and noticed they were covered in dirt. "I guess I really need a bath."

Jamie laughed. "I wasn't going to say anything, but you stink, girlfriend."

"Thanks a lot."

"We'll be back to check on you tomorrow. General Romulus promised me you would be given quarters on board the ship as well as a day or two off to heal properly."

"The nurse said I'd be fully healed by tomorrow morning."

Jamie slapped me on the shoulder and it stung. "Woman, take the day off. Trust me. Speaking of..." She glanced down at a display on her forearm. "We're due for Queen Bitch patrol in half an hour."

"What?" I asked.

Jamie stood and gave me a quick, gentle hug. "You've heard of Queen Raya and her planet-destroying missiles?"

"Yes."

"Well, I'm on missile patrol, saving the galaxy one blown-up missile at a time."

"What happens if you miss one?"

Mia and Jamie both froze, but it was Mia who spoke. "Not funny. Not going to happen. Not on my watch."

Jamie clarified. "Mia finds 'em and I kill 'em. Most of the time. Sometimes I find one first, but that's rare. I'm only one small ship, and Mia has a freaking army of satellites, drones, and scanners."

"My minions are very well trained," Mia agreed.

"They're computers."

"Very well-trained computers."

They walked toward the door but turned to wave farewell. "Get better!" Jamie ordered.

"Give him time." Mia's words were no less an order.

"I'll try."

The door slid open, and I caught the barest glimpse of two men I recognized from their game avatars, Kassius and Alexius. The alien hotties we'd all oohed and ahhed over every time we played.

The only one missing was mine.

"Let's get you ready for the next round of visitors." The nurse's false cheer and wink were appreciated but wasted on me. Maybe it wasn't false, but I didn't know her. She didn't know me. I didn't trust others easily. And when I put weight on my leg, I felt anything but cheery.

"Can we not talk? I'm sorry, but I'm tired, my leg hurts, and I don't feel like saying much."

"Of course." Cheery or not, she was kind. That I appreciated very much as she helped me move, step by agonizing step, toward what appeared to be a shower with a seat in the center.

Thank all that was holy, because there was no way I could stand up long enough to take a shower.

I didn't hear the door open. The nurse turned in alarm, then smiled. "Starfighter Darius, I was wondering when you would appear."

"Now. And I will take care of her."

"Of course." The nurse smiled and nodded her head without the slightest protest. The next thing I knew, I was in Darius's arms, cradled against his chest like a baby. I was wearing an alien version of a hospital gown, which, as most hospital attire was wont to do, didn't cover much.

Darius stopped at the bed and pulled the blanket loose to cover me, tucking me into his arms as gently as he could.

"What are you doing? I'm supposed to take a shower."

"I will take care of you in our private quarters, Lily. I'm here now, and nothing else is going to hurt you tonight."

Except you, I thought, but I laid my head against his shoulder and didn't argue as he carried me.

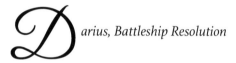

arius, Battleship Resolution

THE ACHE, the guilt of failing my brother, of his death was nothing compared to the thought of losing her. My life. My pair bond. *Mine.*

I held Lily cradled to my chest as I hurried to our quarters. I avoided eye contact with everyone we passed on the battleship, not wanting to stop and talk. Introduce the newest Elite Starfighter from Earth. She was a celebrity. I knew that, logically. The success of the previous two Earth females had ensured Lily's arrival was highly anticipated by all Velerions. Everyone wanted to get a closer look. Meet her. Make her a friend.

The fifth officer who called out a greeting made me

grind my teeth and turn down a less traveled route on the large ship.

I had no patience for others. The medical team had made me wait. General Romulus had made me wait. Lily was in my arms, and I was not stopping until I had her snugly in my bed.

I needed to know, to feel that Lily was safe and whole and alive. Having her heart beating next to mine, holding her, touching her—and soon, being buried deep within her—would be the only way to convince the completely illogical part of me that everything was all right.

My emotions raged out of control. I truly felt like I was the Atlan beast in one of Lily's erotic books. I'd secretly scoffed at the beast character's lack of discipline, his inability to master his physical and emotional need for his mate.

Now who was acting like a wild animal, struggling to speak, to think? Trying to maintain a thin veneer of civility so I would not scare the female I so desperately needed to protect?

I looked at Lily. Her long hair had partially escaped its braid and was now a wild, snarled tangle framing her face. The blanket I'd wrapped her in did not do enough to keep her warm as I walked through the battleship to our temporary quarters. She shivered and I pulled her closer, tighter to my chest.

She gasped in pain.

"Damn Vega, I'm sorry. I didn't mean to hurt you."

"I know. It's okay."

"No. I should have been more careful."

"Nobody's perfect, Darius. I'm fine. In fact, I can't believe you are carrying me. I'm too heavy for this. Don't you people have wheelchairs or something?"

We did, in fact, have mobile chairs that were very efficient. "I want to hold you." I looked straight ahead and willed my heart to stop pounding in terror. She was in my arms. Safe. "I need to feel you."

With a sigh I took for surrender, she settled her head back on my shoulder and made no more attempts to protest. When we arrived at the section of the battleship where they were housing the Titan teams who had fought today, I found Bantia and Ulixes standing outside our door, waiting.

"How is she?" Bantia asked.

"She's fine," Lily answered. "And I'm right here. My ears work just fine."

Bantia laughed, the relief evident in her face. "Thank Vega. I don't know what Darius would have done if—"

"Do not speak of it," I commanded before she could finish. I did not need to hear my fears spoken aloud by another. Having my darkest thoughts shared would amplify my instinct to protect Lily at all costs. I was already fighting the need to lock my pair-bonded female in a room and keep her there, away from battle and cannon fire and explosions of rock burying her alive.

Ulixes inclined his head to my female. "We are very relieved to see you are well."

"Thank you."

He looked at me; our gazes locked as he spoke. "General Romulus has ordered all Titan teams to report tomorrow, after second meal. They have reviewed today's mission and have teams scouring through what's left of the base. He will be giving us a report, and possibly a new mission, tomorrow."

"We won't be there."

Lily stiffened in my arms. "Yes, we will. The doctor—or nurse—whoever she was, said the bone grower robots would have my leg better than new by morning."

"No. You need more than one night to heal."

"According to the doctor, I don't." She looked up at Ulixes. "We'll be there."

"I said no."

Lily's voice sharpened, the crisp cadence of her words becoming extreme. "I will be there. I cannot speak for Darius of Velerion. Perhaps he is planning to retire."

Bantia was covering her mouth, but I could see the laughter in her eyes. I was not amused. "Lily, we will discuss this in private."

"No we won't."

Ulixes cleared his throat and wrapped his arm around his pair-bonded female, gently guiding her back toward what I assumed were their temporary quarters, away from us.

"See you tomorrow," Bantia called over her shoulder.

Lily drew breath to call back, but I lowered my face to hers and kissed her so she could not respond. When I let her up for air, Bantia and Ulixes were nowhere to be seen.

"That wasn't fair."

"When it comes to you, bonded one, I have no intention of playing fair."

Her silence suited me as I carried her into the sparsely furnished soldiers' quarters. There was a bathing unit, clean uniforms laid out for each of us, two meals, drinking water, and nutrition bars on a table no larger than one of the pillows on the bed. I could take care of my pair bonded, bathe her, feed her, and make sure she rested in my arms.

I didn't need anything else. Not tonight.

Carrying her to the table, I settled her in the chair and pulled the foodstuffs toward her, opening everything. "You will eat. All of it."

"You are very bossy."

That made me chuckle, but only because Lily was already taking a bite of the nutrition bar I'd placed in her hand.

"Yum. This almost tastes like watermelon."

I chose another flavor and ate the entire thing in two bites, saving the other bar of the same flavor for her.

"Drink." The water cartridge I set in front of her was full and loaded with minerals and healing amino acids the doctor had assured me she would need to regain her full strength.

She sipped, then set it down. "That's too cold."

I lifted the cartridge, adjusted the temperature setting and handed it back to her. "Try it now."

Eyebrow raised, she lifted the small opening to her lips and sucked more water into her mouth. "How did you do that? It's room temperature now."

Showing her how to adjust the water to her liking, I unwrapped more food and placed it before her, a feeling of intense satisfaction raising my chest as she devoured the food like she was starving.

Odd. I enjoyed caring for her. Seeing her satisfied. Sated, whether in bed from intense orgasms or from the simple act of drinking chilled water.

I'd never behaved this way before, and I had no idea how to stop myself or control the urge.

When she'd had enough, I lifted her and carried her to the bathing unit. There was no tub to recline in, but I pulled a small seat out from its built-in resting place in the wall and set her down. The medical gown was easy to remove, and I set the water stream to warm her. She leaned back with a groan, and I stepped out, quickly stripped, and joined her.

She frowned. "What are you doing?"

I didn't know exactly; I only knew I needed her close to me. I needed to soothe her, care for her, take away her pain.

Her soft skin was smudged by a coating of sweat and dust. She'd been through so much, and yet to me, she looked even more beautiful than the first time I'd seen her.

I knelt at her feet and slowly, gently rubbed the cleanser over her body. When I stood and reached for her hair, she melted into my hold, and I took my time unwinding what was left of her braid and working the cleansing agent through the long strands.

"God, yes," she murmured. "You're hired."

Unable to turn away, to blink, I studied her, hypnotized by her lips, the curve of her cheek, the tender welcome on her face. This was the real Lily. My Lily. Soft. Submissive. Gentle.

The fierce, defiant fighter who had driven me half-mad on the battlefield was gone, replaced by this delicate, serene goddess.

I'd done everything in my power to keep my body from reacting to her, but as she leaned into my touch, every protective, fierce, ruthless instinct I had wanted to mark her. Claim her. Punish her for every terrifying moment I'd spent digging her out of the rubble. Fearing she was dead. Forgetting to breathe. Every cell in my body flooded with guilt and pain at the thought of losing her.

That need to mark her filled my mind and I felt my body grow hard with lust and I closed my eyes, imagined taking her here, now, her hands on the small seat, her bottom in my hands as I pounded into her from behind.

"Well, that's interesting."

I glanced down to find her gaze focused on my hard cock.

"Ignore it. You are not ready."

"Says who? You?" Lifting one hand, she reached for me, wrapping her fingers around my cock and squeezing until my knees nearly buckled.

"Lily, you should not..."

"Bossy, Darius. Too bossy." She ran her thumb along the head, and a shudder ran through my body. "You are tense. I can feel it. Let me take care of you."

"I am taking care of—"

Her mouth closed around my cock, and she slid my length deep. The heat of her made my balls draw up in pain as I fought back an instant release. When she swirled her tongue around my tip and used one of her hot little hands to stroke my balls, I was done.

I exploded, lost control, couldn't stop. Didn't want to stop as I pumped my cock into her mouth, gave her everything.

The release was shattering, emotions making my face heat, my eyes burn. She'd destroyed me in seconds, shattered my control.

"Why? Why did you do that? I'm supposed to be taking care of you." I dropped to my knees before her, ready to pleasure her in kind, but she placed a hand on my cheek and shook her head.

"I'm too tired, Darius. I hurt. I just want to go to bed."

Unwilling, perhaps unable to deny her anything, I rinsed her hair and turned off the water. I dried her gently, then left her for a few moments to take care of her personal needs while I dried myself and pulled down the soft bedding and fluffed her pillow. I felt completely out of my element until the door slid open and she was there, the curve of her body perfectly silhouetted by the light coming from behind her. Curves everywhere. Softness. Mine.

She was mine. If I had to feed her by hand, bathe her, and carry her to bed, I would. Every damn day.

I closed the distance at once and wrapped an arm around her waist so I could lead her to the bed. Once I settled her in place and lay down next to her, I pulled her into my arms and gently placed her injured leg on top of mine. Her soft sigh of pleasure made my chest tighten.

"Oh, you're so warm."

She snuggled in close, and I covered us with the soft bedding. Her eyes were already closed when I gave the command that plunged the room into darkness.

Lily slept for hours. I held her and replayed every moment of the day's failed mission, determined that next time, no matter what I had to do, I *would* keep her safe.

Even if she hated me for it.

ily

I COULD GET USED to this. Soft bed. Even softer sheets. Darius wrapped around me, his arm tucked snuggly around my waist, his chest at my back. I'd never felt so safe, so languid. I didn't want to move. Ever.

"How is your leg feeling?" Darius kissed the back of my head but didn't move otherwise.

My leg. I'd completely forgotten.

Timid at first, then with growing confidence when I didn't want to cry with pain, I moved my leg. The muscles felt sore, like I'd done a few too many squats the day before, but otherwise I felt great. The deep agony I'd suffered buried under that rock was gone. A memory.

Not one I wished to dwell on, let alone repeat, now that my leg was healed. "The doctor was right. The pain is gone. I guess the bone must be healed."

Darius moved his hand from my waist to my thigh and explored the thin bandage that still covered the surgical site, lightly massaging the muscle. I melted. Like, puddle of hot wax melted.

"That feels good."

"Does it?" He continued to run his hot hand up and down my thigh, massaging and squeezing the muscle, making sure I was well. When I sighed and rolled onto my back to face him, I discovered the room was too dark to make out his expression.

"What time is it?" I asked. How was a woman supposed to figure out what time of day it was in outer space? Worse, on a ship in outer space. No sunrise. No sunset. No birds singing or insects making noise. No cars or honking horns. Our room was dark and silent except for a gentle hum that seemed to be coming from the very walls, the floor itself. I assumed that had to be from something mechanical on the ship. Engines? Water pumps? I had no idea.

"Time?"

Darius spoke loudly, and the ship answered. "Ship time zero nine zero seven."

"Is that morning?"

He smiled at me. "Yes, bonded one. Are you hungry? Do you want to go eat something?"

"Later." I lifted my hand to his face and searched for

what I wanted. His lips. "Right now I want you to kiss me."

His hand froze in place on my leg. "I'll want more than a kiss."

"So do I." I wanted *him.* Touching me. Inside me. Hot skin all over mine. I wanted to breathe him in and taste him and feel alive. Feel something other than fear and pain and weakness. I didn't want to think about broken bones or battle or explosions.

When I tangled my fingers in the hair at the back of his neck and pulled him toward me in the dark, he didn't resist. The clash of our lips, our tongues, was a frenzied claiming.

Moments later Darius had pressed my back to the bed. He tore his lips from mine and kissed my cheek. My neck. Lower. When he reached my hard nipples, my back arched off the bed. So sensitive. So *alive.*

He moved lower, the lightest graze of his lips over my clit, a gentle kiss before he moved to my injured leg. "Light, level four."

The room brightened, and I closed my eyes in protest. "Hey!"

"I need to see for myself."

Brilliant. I was naked, bared to the room, fighting the urge to cover myself, and Darius leaned close to inspect the bandaged area of my thigh.

Ready to tell him to leave it, the words caught in my throat when he leaned down and kissed the center of the bandage. "What are you doing?"

"Taking care of you."

Closing my eyes, I turned my head away. It hurt to watch him as he placed kiss after kiss over the suddenly hypersensitive area. Other than the staff nurses at my various boarding schools, who spent half of their time bandaging a skinned knee and the other half chastising a young lady for being a tomboy, I couldn't remember anyone ever taking care of me but me.

When I couldn't take it anymore, I reached for him. "Darius."

"Impatient, are we?" He grinned up at me, then moved so that his chin was poised above my wet core. "Can I kiss you here?"

"Yes."

"Are you sure?"

"Tease."

His gaze locked to mine, and he slid two fingers inside me, the desire in his eyes holding me prisoner. "Is this what you want?"

"More."

With a grin I could only describe as male satisfaction, he lowered his mouth to me and sucked the sensitive bits into his mouth, played me with his tongue, and fucked me with his fingers until I was begging. "Please."

"Come for me."

"You're. So—"

His fingers went deep. Twisted and rubbed a sensitive place I didn't even know I had. I cried out as an orgasm ripped through me.

"Bossy!"

He didn't stop, moving and tasting until I was spent before kissing his way up my body. I reached for him as he settled between my thighs and his hard cock sank into my wet heat with an agonizing slowness that made the sensitive inner muscles spasm again.

I gripped his shoulders. My hips rose to take more of him. Demanded more. His control was like iron, and he moved in and out of me with a slow, steady pace that pushed me higher and higher until another orgasm sent my body into spasms, taking me by surprise.

With a groan that sounded like my name, he moved. Hard. Fast. Out of control. I moved with him, taking everything he had and wanting more. Always more.

We both exploded, his body shuddering over mine with an intensity that shocked me.

He covered me when it was over, and I welcomed the warm weight of him, just enough to make me feel protected but most of his weight on his arms.

"You are dangerous," he said.

The compliment pleased me, and I stroked his back with every ounce of emotion I wasn't ready to name, let alone speak aloud.

For long minutes we remained entwined, neither of us ready to move until forced to abandon the few moments of bliss.

Eventually reality invaded my thoughts. Food. Shower. Mission briefing. More fighting.

Darius must have felt the tension in my limbs,

because he rolled to the side, pulling me with him. When I was tucked under his shoulder, he sighed. "Can we stay here all day?"

"You know we can't."

"I don't want you fighting today, Lily. It's too soon."

I didn't argue. We still had time to be together, like this. I didn't want to waste a single moment.

arius, five hours later

THE MISSION BRIEFING room onboard *Battleship Resolution* was not quite as big as the room we used at Arturri, but there was ample seating for the seven Titan teams, a handful of Starfighter pilots and Lily's friend Mia and her pair bonded, Kassius, our only full Starfighter-level mission control specialists.

Lily's other human friend, Jamie, an Elite Starfighter pilot, sat next to us on Lily's right with her pair bonded, Alexius.

As the women had shortened their males' names to Kass and Alex, I'd begun thinking of them the same way. We'd all shared a meal prior to this meeting, during which Alex had told me my name should be shortened to Earth speak as well and they would all call me *Dar*.

Thank Vega Lily had told them all an instant no. Saved me beating the other Starfighters into giving that one up. Kass and Alex had both laughed at her protest, but I had a feeling if I were ever alone with them, they would call me Dar just to poke at me. Which was fine. I wasn't above forgetting the *K* sound at the beginning of Kass's name. I hadn't come up with ideas for Alex yet, but I would. We were family now, as our pair-bonded females considered one another sisters, per Lily. If they were important to Lily, they were important to me.

"Starfighters, we have an unexpected opportunity before us." General Romulus paced the front of the room as the wall behind him became a massive screen.

At that moment the meeting room door slid open and General Aryk, General Jennix, and two Elite Starfighter pilots I did not recognize entered the room. General Romulus looked at General Aryk, who gave an imperceptible nod. He, in turn, gave a silent signal to Mia and Kass, who stood.

"All right. Starfighters MCS Mia Becker and Kassius Remeas will take over from here."

Lily's friends walked to the front of the meeting room and pulled up a nav grid that appeared to show placements of a large fleet of Queen Raya's forces massing just beyond the planet Xenon's moon.

"Is that a Dark Fleet cruiser?" A voice from the back

of the room brought all chatter to a halt, the room suddenly eerily silent.

"Yes." Mia pointed to a small dot near the corner of the nav grid. "And it's not the only one. There are three cruisers in the attack formation."

Lily leaned forward, squinting a bit to try to make out the ship Mia was pointing to. From our seats the small image was difficult to see clearly, no more than a dot on the wall. Otherwise she seemed unaffected. Unlike me. I knew how powerful those ships were. How massive. Dangerous.

A ship like that had killed my brother.

Lily looked at Mia. "So, are we going to go take them out or what?"

My chest tightened at the idea of Lily getting anywhere near one of those ships, and I answered her question. "No, we are not."

Lily held up her hand, elbow on the table in front of us, palm turned toward me. "I didn't ask you, Darius. Mia?"

"We have reason to believe that Queen Raya is on the third cruiser."

"That's not enough reason to attack. We'll lose too many fighters." That same voice from the back. I glanced over my shoulder to see Elite Starfighter Pilot Ryzix and his pair-bonded partner, Gustar. They flew the *Lanix*. I had met them a long time ago but hadn't seen them since my brother's death. They were very skilled. Highly respected. Merciless in a fight.

Neither one looked at all pleased at the prospect of taking on one Dark Fleet cruiser. But three? I was in complete agreement. It was a suicide mission.

Kass waited for the mumbles of agreement to die down before speaking. "We also have reason to believe Queen Raya's forces are amassing in preparation for a direct assault on Velerion."

The stillness was so profound I could hear my own heartbeat.

"When?" Jamie asked.

"In two days," Mia said.

Up to this point in the war, Queen Raya had not dared assault our planet directly. She'd struck at our former Starfighter base, but that had not been located on our planet's surface. Velerion's satellite defense grid was formidable. When combined with the Starfighters stationed on Moon Base Arturri, our ground-to-air forces on the surface, and the Velerion space fleet, a direct assault on the home planet was unthinkable.

"Is this a joke? Because this is not amusing." This time it was the golden-haired Gustar who had spoken. We all waited for Kass or Mia to respond. I hoped, prayed this information, wherever they had acquired it, was wrong. But when I looked at Mia's drawn, worried expression, my heart sank into my boots.

This was no joke. And we, all of Velerion, were in serious trouble.

Mia adjusted the nav grid, enlarging sections as she detailed their intelligence. Queen Raya's Dark Fleet allies, disturbed by her recent defeats, first at the hex port and then on the colony planet of Xenon, had decided the incoming Starfighter trainees from Earth posed too large a threat to their war efforts. To mitigate that threat, they were choosing to launch a direct assault on Velerion now, presumably before any more Starfighters from other worlds could join the fight.

I didn't bother to ask how Queen Raya knew about Jamie or Mia. I knew Jamie had spent time as the queen's prisoner. And like any other ruler, she had spies everywhere. Not to mention that the success of the Starfighter Training Academy program on Earth was big news on Velerion. It wasn't exactly a secret, not after the first two Starfighters to arrive had won such decisive victories. Jamie had been captured, escaped, and managed to save an entire planet from an IPBM attack. Mia had helped plan and coordinate the successful attack on Xenon station and disabled the Dark Fleet's primary communication and defense system on that planet's moon.

Jamie and Mia had been too fucking good.

"We believe the bunker on Xenon was a trap designed to eliminate our newest Starfighter Titan, Lily Becker of Earth," General Romulus added from where he stood to the side of the nav grid. "They knew we would deploy the Titan teams to that location. Not only was the interior wired to blow, but the cliffs had been drilled to ensure anyone in that area would be buried under massive rockslides."

Lily leaned forward, an angry glare on her face. "Are you telling me they set that whole thing up for me?"

Mia looked her dead in the eye. "Yes."

"That's insane."

"And yet you survived," the general pointed out. "Elite Starfighters are powerful. You are no exception."

"But—"

I placed my hand on her thigh and gently squeezed. Lily blinked rapidly, shaking her head. To me she whispered, "I'm a librarian, Darius. This is crazy. How do they even know about me?"

"Spies."

"Brilliant."

"They were nearly successful in killing not only Lily, but several members of the Titan teams," Kass added. "Three Titan fighters remain in medical. Lily, your Titan, Athena, was destroyed. They are building you a new one, but it won't be ready for several days, and we don't have that long."

Was I an ass for breathing a sigh of relief at the news? I did not want my Lily in another battle so soon after I'd nearly lost her. The medics said her leg was healed, but that did nothing to calm me or my need to protect her.

My relief was short-lived.

"Elite Starfighter Titan Divi suffered severe burns during the battle on Xenon. She is still in the medical station, sedated, as her skin regenerates. Her second-tier bonded fighter, her sister Dea, spoke briefly with Divi this morning, and she has agreed to transfer her Titan, *Bellator,* to Lily for use in this battle."

"Athena was completely destroyed? Wreckage?" Lily looked heartbroken.

"She saved your life, and she is being rebuilt," Mia assured her. "She just won't be ready for this mission."

Lily sat back, her arms crossed over her chest. As Mia adjusted the images again, Lily turned to me. "Sisters? I didn't know we could be siblings."

I shrugged. "Off-world pairings have always been pair-bonded, but not all partnerships are. Some are siblings. Best friends. Anyone you fight well with and are willing to die to protect."

"Except your brother died and you didn't."

The cutting voice came from nearby. I closed my eyes as the familiar guilt and pain swelled in my throat, burning its way in two directions to make both my chest and my head ache.

"What?" Lily turned around. "Who said that?"

"Lily." Mia cleared her throat and Lily faced forward to listen, but her gaze repeatedly darted to me, the accusation I saw there one I could not deny. I had not told her everything, that was true. But I'd done it to protect her.

Mia and Kass detailed the mission. Queen Raya's fleet was set up for multiple waves of attack. First would be drones to take out Velerion's satellite defense grid. Thousands of them. Followed by waves of Scythe fighters clearing a pathway for ground troop deployment via shuttle drops. The cruisers were going to triangulate multiphase and multifrequency jammers so we would have direct line of sight, laser communication only.

It was going to be a complete fucking nightmare.

And then General Romulus spoke directly to the Titan teams.

"According to intel, Queen Raya will be orbiting near Velerion's equator on this cruiser." He pointed to a large ship. "Our plan is to take one Titan team to each cruiser before they arrive in Velerion space. The Titan teams will deploy from a stealth shuttle that will use Xenon's magnetic field to hide their presence and remain just outside their scanner range. When the cruisers pass Xenon on their way here, those Titan teams will rely on ejection velocity and their own boosters to navigate and attach to the cruisers' hulls."

"Holy fuck."

Ryzix again, and I completely agreed. The Titans would be hurtling through space with no support team, no backup, no way out if they didn't make it, and not enough air or reserve fuel to return to Velerion any way but on one of those cruisers' hulls.

Titans could fly, but the external shielding couldn't handle the heat and stress of planetary re-entry. Nor did the Titans have enough energy reserve to make that kind of landing or wait for another ride home.

"We have analyzed their attack strategy. If they succeed in placing the cruisers in orbit, Velerion will fall." General Aryk, our highest-ranking officer in the fleet and leader of the Galactic Alliance, paused for a long minute to let that sink in.

"So, how do we stop them?" Lily asked. "The shuttle shoots one of us out like a cannonball, we adjust on the fly using our boosters, grab onto the cruiser hull, and then what? Won't they know the second we land?"

Mia shook her head. "No. The Titans are too small. As far as their ship is concerned, you'll be space debris, a pebble bouncing off the hull. Even their defense system will ignore you until you start tearing things apart."

"But we do get to tear them to pieces?"

"Absolutely."

Lily made an odd gesture with her hand in a rolling motion that caused Mia to smile as she continued. "Once the Titan team attaches to the cruiser hull, you will target one of the two grav generators that power their thrusters." She adjusted the nav grid screen so that a schematic drawing of the cruiser filled the entire wall. Mia pointed to two distinct areas on the cruiser's exterior. "Here's where things get dicey."

"Dicey?" I asked Lily.

"Dangerous."

I grunted. As if the rest of the mission up to this point was not.

"The Titans will be carrying modified IPBM triggers recovered from the production facility on Xenon. The triggers are not as powerful as full IPBMs, but will be more than enough to start a chain reaction that will cripple the ship, perhaps even destroy it."

"And how does the Titan team evacuate?" I asked.

"Booster reserves will be used to launch the Titan toward a previously designated set of coordinates where you will await retrieval by a shuttle." General Romulus's tone did not invite comment. "The Titans have a critical role to play in ending this war. The Starfighter pilots will be needed to engage with the Scythe fighters. Our MCS team and their support crews will be working to hack into the attack drones' communication systems as well as fight to keep our satellites and comms operations. Shuttle pilots will be evacuating civilian targets as well as moving ground forces and supplies. Our entire fleet has been recalled and ordered into defensive positions around Velerion, the moon, and Xenon to protect our people and repel the attack. We cannot lose this fight. Do you understand?"

Dea, the Titan whose sister was recovering from burns, spoke softly. "What about our families on the surface? Does the public know? Can we call them? Warn them?"

"Not yet. Queen Raya is being very careful to keep her ships in the dark zones, outside of our normal scan or patrol areas. If we alert the public too soon, her spies will report back that we are aware of the attack. As of right now, the only people who know are in this room, and it needs to stay that way until we have Titans in place on those cruisers."

Dea nodded. "When do we leave?"

General Romulus inclined his head to Dea in respect

and thanks. "I have already spoken to several Titans who have volunteered for the mission. We need six Titans. With your addition, we have five."

"I'll go," Lily offered before I could stop her. "I volunteer, assuming I can take your sister's Titan?" She looked at Dea, who nodded.

"Of course. She would be honored."

"No."

Lily turned to me. "You don't control me, Darius."

"You are not going on that mission." I looked up at General Romulus. "I'll go instead."

The general shook his head. "Negative. The mission positions are assigned and filled. You will report with the rest of the Titans tomorrow at twelve forty to go over ground support on Velerion."

"No."

"Are you refusing a direct order?"

Fuck. Fuck. Fuck. "No, General, but respectfully, it doesn't make sense to split up a pair-bonded team. They work better together, more instinctively. I should go."

"I've already spoken to Dea's family. Provided she volunteered, I told them she would be mission approved. I understand you were just pair-bonded, but you'll have to sit this one out."

I stared into General Romulus's eyes. Fuck, I hated politics. There would be no mission beside his pair bond. The General had made the decision before entering the room. I straightened. "Very well."

"Excellent. Titans heading for the cruisers, be back

here at zero eight twenty tomorrow. We'll go over the ordinance and booster fuel options. Mission details will be available to each of you on your personal devices. Study them. Memorize everything. You launch at ten, sharp." He looked around the room. "This is the end, Starfighters. We live or we die. But we fight to the end."

A collective shout went around the room. I raised my voice with the rest, but I could not accept what had just happened. And Lily? She stood, turned on her heel, and walked away from me without a backward glance.

What the fuck was happening here? How was I supposed to protect her if she fought me at every turn? This was unacceptable.

Lily was going on the most dangerous mission I could ever imagine. Alone. And there wasn't a damn thing I could do to stop her.

I glanced over my shoulder to watch the Starfighter Titan, Dea, speaking to one of the pilots.

Maybe there was something I could do after all.

ily

"LIAR. LIAR. BLOODY LIAR!" I took my favorite romance novel off the shelf, the book with my all-time favorite, sexy, honorable, *respectful* alien warrior hero, my Atlan beast, and threw the damn thing across the room.

Reached for another. I'd brought two with me on this mission, thinking that maybe I would share them with Darius and try out some of the more interesting sexual antics. Hadn't needed them. Still.

I glanced down at the graphic, the title, the dream.

This cover was so sexy. It would be a shame...

No. Nope. *Goddamn it*. When I got back to the moon base on Arturri, I was going to toss the rest of them.

"Grace Goodwin, you bitch. I am going to have words with you when I get home." This author was a liar. There was no sexy alien hunk out here in space waiting to make all my dreams come true.

They weren't big dreams, either. At least I didn't think so. I wanted someone to love me, respect me, and believe in me. Believe in my capabilities. My courage. My brain. All I wanted was someone to have faith that I was capable of winning. Creating. Being more than what I appeared to be on my average, mousy, introverted exterior.

But noooo. In fact, Darius was so dead set against me going on this mission, he'd defied General Romulus and *humiliated me* in front of *every* Starfighter on the battleship, *three* generals, *and* my best friends.

Oh no! Delicate little flower Lily can't go on that super *dangerous mission. She'll die! We'll all die! Oh me, oh my, General Romulus, you need to send me instead. I'm a* big, tough warrior. *I can do it for her. Poor little Lily. She needs protection. She just doesn't know how* fragile *she is.*

Asshole.

And he'd been lying to me since I met him. I'd been so trusting, so blinded by orgasms and the promise of someone who actually cared about me, believed in me, *chose me,* that I didn't ask. Didn't want to know.

Well, a few quick questions after the mission briefing and a computer search later and I'd learned the truth on my own.

I wasn't Darius's first choice. Tycho, his brother, had been his fighting partner for three years. Three. Years.

He'd died on a mission not long before I started playing *Starfighter Training Academy.* Perhaps a few weeks before I'd selected Darius, from all the game's options, to be my partner on missions in game.

I'd been playing a game. Darius had been looking for a way to redeem himself and get back into a Starfighter uniform.

He and his brother had disobeyed a direct order. Jeopardized multiple team members. Most of the mission details were redacted, but I knew enough. Tycho had been killed, and Darius had been kicked out of the Titan program.

Until me. Until I beat the game—training simulation, whatever the fuck these aliens wanted to call it—and earned each of us a place inside a Titan.

I wasn't important to him. I was a means to an end with a dose of on-demand sex on the side.

No wonder he hadn't told me the truth about his past, his brother. Any of it.

I fought back tears and stared at the book in my hand. "I should have gone to Atlan, yeah?"

After this mission, I was going home. I had no reason to stay. Once Velerion was safe and the evil super villain, Queen Raya, was dead or captured or whatever was going to happen to her, I was leaving this shithole life behind. I didn't care about this war. As long as children weren't dying and some evil bitch wasn't ruining the lives of innocent people on this planet, I was out. Conscience clear.

Done.

Finished.

The sex with Darius was great, no doubt. Better than I'd ever imagined it could be. But I'd been treated like a failure my entire life. Made to feel like I didn't *quite* measure up. If I lost ten pounds, my mother encouraged me to lose five more. A master's degree? Wonderful, but Connie Winthrop had a PhD. Ooh-la-la. And her sister? Penelope? Well, darling, she married into a barony and already had her third child on the way. Wasn't that wonderful?

Totally, completely fucking wonderful, mum.

Too bad I couldn't change my name to Penelope and manage, for once in my life, to please my mother. In preparing to come here, to leave Earth behind, I'd written them a cryptic letter and left my bills on autopay. Guess deep down I'd known this wasn't going to work out.

I wasn't going to fight this battle with Darius. I deserved better. More.

He didn't have to love me. I could deal with that. But I would not tolerate being mollycoddled and disrespected. Treated like a child who didn't know better.

I was *not* going to cry.

The door to our temporary quarters slid open, and Darius appeared seconds later at the entrance to the small bedroom. Soon to be *his* bedroom. Solo. I'd already made arrangements to sleep elsewhere tonight. My own room. This ship had hundreds.

"I need to speak to you."

"Really? Now you want to talk?" I looked down at the

fantasy man on the cover of the novel I held and shook my head. "No. I don't want to talk to you."

"You aren't going on that mission, Lily. I forbid it."

What. The. Fuck?

"You forbid it?" I heard the high, lilting quality of my voice and made no attempt to adjust. I was pretty sure Darius had no idea what that tone meant. He was about to find out.

"It's too dangerous."

"Is it?" I pulled the sleeve that had been partially covering the comm unit on my wrist and looked at the message I'd received from General Romulus not five minutes ago, verifying that the meeting details for tomorrow's mission launch were still there. That I hadn't imagined it.

"Tell General Romulus you changed your mind. I will take your place."

I stood slowly, holding the Grace Goodwin book, the total goddamn lie, and walked to a disposal unit that would send the paper to recycling. Dropped the story inside. Closed it. "I'm going. My flight simulation scores were higher than yours. I have a better chance of reaching that cruiser alive, and you know it. Besides, Queen Raya tried to kill me with a rockslide. Not you."

"I can't let you do this, Lily."

"No?" I picked up the book I'd thrown on the floor and walked to the disposal unit. Threw the second book inside. *Bye-bye, beast.* "Can't? Really? Like you can't tell me the truth. Like you didn't tell me you had a brother die? Your second-tier bonded fighting partner? Tycho?"

"There was never a good time." He had the good sense to look ashamed of himself.

"Uh-huh." I walked to the small seating area outside the bedroom and marveled that even here, on a battleship, in outer space, the Starfighter quarters were much nicer than anything I'd ever seen in a movie, at least on a naval ship of any kind.

"Lily, are you listening to me?"

"Totally. Please, keep talking." I took a seat on the small sofa-style bench, lifted the water I'd been drinking earlier from a small table, and finished it off.

"Lily..." He paused, ran his fingers through his hair, that gorgeous, soft hair I'd been tugging on just hours ago, as if he suddenly didn't know what to say.

"No, Darius. Go ahead. Tell me why you *humiliated* me in front of three generals, every Starfighter on this ship, and my friends. Tell me how dangerous this mission is. How worried you are about me. How weak and unskilled and incapable I am. Go ahead. I've heard it all before."

"Stop. I didn't say any of those things."

"Didn't you?" I set the now-empty water jug down slowly. Deliberately. My tone was detached. Calm. My mother had trained me well. "I'm going on this mission, and then I'm going home. I'm sure you'll be able to find a new partner in no time, now that you're back in an Elite Starfighter uniform."

My eyes were burning. Tears. No. No. No. I blinked them away and took a deep breath to clear my head. "I've already made arrangements to stay elsewhere tonight. We're finished. Done. You don't owe me anything."

I stood and walked the three steps to the door.

Don't look back.

Don't look back.

I did, to see Darius's pale face. Round eyes. He looked shocked. Unsure. I almost felt sorry for him. Almost.

"I'm sorry about your brother."

Darius still hadn't moved when I exited the small room, the door sliding closed on a past that was too painful to dwell on. I had a mission to complete, a planet to save.

I was a goddamn Elite Starfighter Titan, not a sappy schoolgirl.

To hell with external validation. With needing approval from other people. I had completed the training program. I'd been chosen. Mia and Jamie were friends I'd chosen, friends who respected me and treated me well. Supported me and my decisions.

I was done giving others so much power over me, my emotions, my confidence.

"I'm a badass bitch."

I rounded the corner to find Bantia there, smiling. "Indeed you are." She held a hand to her chest and gave me a little bow. "So, you are taking on one of the cruisers with Dea tomorrow."

"I am."

"Last one to blow up their cruiser has to buy the victory drinks."

"Deal."

I held out my hand, and she took it, grinned when I squeezed her hand and moved our clasped palms up and down to seal the agreement.

"I have to warn you, I'm not cheap. I like the good stuff from the Andromeda system."

"I'm not worried. You'll be buying."

We both smiled and released our hold. I walked past her and continued on so I could explore the rest of the ship. If this was my last night in outer space, I wanted to see more of it than a bedroom.

———

Darius

GENERAL ROMULUS WAS WAITING for me when I knocked on the door to his private quarters.

"I wondered when you'd show up."

"You have to send me on that mission. I'll take Dea's place. I can't do this again. If you won't stop Lily, I have to go with her."

The general looked me over, head to toe, but did not invite me in. "And why would I allow that? Dea is an exceptionally skilled Titan."

"So am I."

"And Lily?"

"You know she's incredible."

"And is that why you implied otherwise at the mission briefing?"

"I didn't—"

He raised a brow. "Perhaps that is why your pair-bonded female has formally requested your bond be severed and erased from the Hall of Records? Has, in fact, told me of her intention to resign and return to Earth? Because you spoke so highly of her to your peers?"

"What?" Lily gone? That was not acceptable. She was mine. Mine to love. Protect. Cherish.

"Indeed. I thought, perhaps, she had decided to keep that information to herself. That would appear to be a trend in your relationship."

"Fuck." His words were daggers to my gut. Lily had said the same thing. That I'd embarrassed her, humiliated her, lied to her. Kept secrets. I needed to keep her safe. That was all. But I'd fucked things up. Badly. I'd just have to talk sense to her, then not let her out of bed until she promised to listen. "Where is she staying tonight? I need to see her."

"I don't believe that particular activity will be on your schedule tonight."

"Where is she?"

He shrugged and I wanted to punch him. Again. As I had the day my brother died. Like that day, striking at the general would not help me protect Lily.

Tycho had been a grown man. He'd made his choices.

Lily made hers. I had to respect that. I couldn't make the same mistake again, or I'd lose her, too. My pair bond. She was everything now. Everything that mattered.

"Please, General. Where is she? I totally fucked this up."

He studied me long and hard. Although he was only a few years older, the burden of his command made him feel more like a father figure than his age probably deserved. Still, the weight of his judgment made my fists clench at my sides.

"Ask Dea. If she will agree to allow you to take her place, I will approve it. On one condition."

"Anything."

"You bring Lily back alive."

ily, Titan Bellator, Launch Shuttle, Deep Space

"CALL ME TOR, Starfighter. I am honored to serve with you."

"Thank you." I didn't know what else to say. I'd used the Titan's full name, Bellator, and been gently corrected. "You can call me Lily."

"Very well." The Titan's deep, masculine voice sounded older than the profile I'd chosen for *Athena*. Almost like a wise, caring father who had raised ten children and seen everything. Tor's voice was soothing. Calm. Like having my own, personal, Captain Jean-Luc Picard on board.

As Tor was the only company I was going to have for

the next few hours, I was happy to discover he didn't sound like a mechanical hag or petulant teen. Some of the voice options when building a Titan were, in my opinion, highly questionable.

"Starfighter, loading has commenced."

"Copy that." I didn't really feel the Titan being loaded onto the launch rail system, not like I had on the planet Xenon. But then, we were in the middle of nowhere, in outer space, with no gravity, no light. Nothing. A few stars were twinkling here and there. I knew once I launched I'd be able to see the planets Velerion, Xenon and Xandrax off in the distance. But they weren't going to be large. More like spotting a spoon across the room from ten meters.

Dea and I were going to be alone out here.

The thought made me wish Darius was here. I shoved that aside and watched the countdown on the display screen in the corner of my helmet.

"Launch sequence has commenced."

"Ready for launch."

The shuttle crew had been efficient and experienced. I was launching first. Dea, who I had not seen since the ordinance meeting back on the battleship, would be launched about half an hour behind me but arrive at nearly the exact same time. We were being hurtled through space onto opposite sides of the Dark Fleet Cruiser. Which meant the shuttle had to travel a fair distance to achieve the appropriate angle of attack for her because we were so very far away.

Dea had stayed in her bunk, which was fine with me. I wasn't in the mood for talking to anyone. I just wanted to do my job and go home to sulk, eat ice cream and curse men in general, but one man in particular.

"Launch in ten…"

I waited.

"Five, four, three, two, one, launch."

There was little difference in the feeling of weightlessness between the shuttle launch bay and hurtling through space at hundreds of kilometers an hour. Perhaps thousands. I wasn't sure about the conversion rates. But it was fast. And as soon as I confirmed my trajectory and activated my boosters, I'd be what I could only call asteroid speed.

Too fast. One speck of space dust could throw a spanner in the works. Blow me to pieces.

"Quit your whining." I was speaking to myself, but Tor appeared to be confused.

"I am unfamiliar with the term."

"I was talking to myself."

"Of course."

"Have you confirmed our current trajectory? Are we on target to attach to the Cruiser?"

"Of course."

"Brilliant. Have you sent the calculations to the shuttle?"

"Of course."

What the everloving hell? "Stop saying *of course.*"

Tor did not speak to me, rather a stream of letters appeared on my helmet's display. Two words.

'Of course.'

I was still laughing when the shuttle crew's transmission reached me. "Lily, we have received and verified your course. Plus shut down communications and proceed with booster fire."

"Confirmed. Going dark." I had to appear to be a piece of rock, space junk, and nothing more or the Dark Fleet Cruiser's defense systems would obliterate me before I even got close.

"Good luck."

"You, too."

I instructed Tor to shut down all non-essential systems, scanners, targeting, communications. Everything but navigation and life support. "Two minute booster burn in three, two, one...burn."

The slight increase in heat around my legs and the internal sound of the booster firing were the only things that registered. I was in a black, lifeless void. I had no sense of time or place. Nothing to look at or study or feel. I didn't feel real.

Watching the timer and the booster fuel readouts kept me sane as time became oddly abstract. I wasn't normally one to suffer from claustrophobia, but my heart rate picked up and the air inside the Titan was suddenly much too hot.

Seconds later the boosters shut down and the standard temperature returned to the cockpit.

"You may speak, Tor."

"Of course."

I tried not to smile and failed. "How long until we arrive at the Cruiser?"

"At current speed, three hours, twenty-two minutes and sixteen seconds."

Trapped in a tin can, shooting through space with massive bombs strapped to my Titan's body was more of a mental challenge than I'd expected. Damn it.

"Tor, have you ever heard of chess?"

"One moment."

I waited as he searched his onboard database. He wasn't allowed to contact any of Velerion's communications or data systems either.

"I have references to chess as a game played on Earth. However, I have no other information."

"Of course...not." Take *that*.

"Would you like to play a game to pass the time?"

"God yes. And please turn off my video. Do you have something else I can look at? Plants or flowers or people? Anything but empty, black space?"

"Of course."

This time I sighed with relief at his two word response. Felt like I could breathe when photos I assumed were from the surface of Velerion began to fade in and out on my monitors. Children playing, mostly. Which was perfect. "Thank you."

"The game of Tabula is popular on Velerion. Would you like me to teach you how to play?"

"Of course." Was I being cheeky? No. Not me. Never.

Tor placed an electronic board on my screen and proceeded to explain a game very similar to backgammon.

We played for hours. Tabula. Another game similar to chess with an odd name.

I didn't win once. But I also didn't hyperventilate thinking about the fact that I was a speck of space dust on a suicide mission. So, I considered that a win.

Nothing, however, could keep my mind off Darius. He'd appeared at the mission briefing today, sat in the back and didn't interfere or approach me. Which was, technically, a victory, as he was respecting my desire not to speak to him. But winning had never felt more like losing. Worse, I couldn't shut down the memories. His touch. The sound of his voice. The way he smelled. His smile. The way I felt as my body exploded when he was inside me.

Every time I thought of him, I hurt. My heart. My soul. Every cell in my body. So why couldn't I just stop? Why didn't I *want* to stop?

"Because you love him, you idiot. You fell in love with him and pissed the whole situation."

"I am unsure of the reference, Lily. How can I help?" Tor asked.

"You can't. Apologies. I was talking to myself again."

"Of course."

I grinned. Those two words were rapidly becoming my favorite bit of comic relief. I understood why Divi, his normal Starfighter partner, hadn't ordered him to stop saying it.

"How much longer?" I felt like the child in the back of the car asking *'when will we get there?'* every few minutes.

"Three minutes."

"What?"

"Five minutes, fifty-four seconds."

"Damn it! Tor! Why didn't you tell me?"

"You asked me not to speak of it until we had arrived."

Good Lord. "Well, this is close enough. Shut all this shit down and give me visuals."

"Of course."

Games disappeared and my screens activated. My view had changed dramatically.

Xenon's moon was clearly visible, the size of a tea cup saucer directly ahead. Behind that, filling nearly my entire screen was the planet Xenon itself.

"How far away is that moon?" I could see it, but with my sensors and comms off, I had no nav grid or point of reference other than the video coming directly from the Titan's exterior cameras to my monitor. "Do we have enough booster fuel to reach it?"

"If my calculations are correct, negative. We are well beyond booster range, even at full capacity."

Well, that wasn't good news, but that is what I'd been told by Mia in the briefing. She's said this moon was a lot bigger than Earth's, and Xenon, larger still.

In space, the size of things seemed oddly irrelevant. Everything was so massive as to be beyond true comprehension. The place was huge. I could see it, but there was no way in hell I would be able to get there.

"What if we just kept going? Could I make it? Use my boosters to land?"

"My external shielding is not designed to survive the plasma burn that would result from entering the planet's atmosphere."

"What about the moon?"

"Our current trajectory would not intersect with the moon's orbit."

Okay. So, no, no, no and fuck no. We were out here with nowhere to go if this cruiser destruction plan didn't work out.

"Where is the Cruiser? Have you found it?"

"Of course."

"Show me." The command was wasted as Tor had shifted and magnified the nav grid as well as created a green targeting lock on an object that looked about the size of my thumbnail on the monitor. But it was growing rapidly. I watched in silence, trying to see the shape I was expecting, the ship I'd been shown in the mission briefings.

We moved closer. Closer. Until something unlike anything I'd seen before in the training filled half my screen.

"We will impact the enemy ship in two minutes."

Impact was the right word. I'd been worried about missing, but the ship was almost as big as Xenon's moon. "That doesn't look like the Cruiser I saw earlier."

"Correct. That is not a Xandraxian Cruiser."

"Then what is it?" The ship was multiple shades of black, each surface reflecting the light from Vega in a different direction. It looked like a sandspur from hell.

"A Dark Fleet Battlestar."

"What does that mean for the mission?"

"Unknown. The Velerion fleet has never encountered one in battle."

"Tell me everything you know in the next sixty seconds."

"Historically, the Battlestar has been used by Dark Fleet operators during planetary invasions. The ship is a polygon with twelve distinct sections. Each section is capable of breaking away from the core and attacking individually once the ship reaches its destination."

"That thing breaks into pieces?"

"Twelve attack vessels and the core." Tor continued as the individual spikes, long blade-like structures two or three times larger than the skyscrapers I'd seen on a visit to New York City, came closer and closer.

"Each attack vessel is an equilateral equiangular polygon with independent navigation, power and weapons systems."

"Can you speak English, please? It looks like a compass star, but meaner."

"I am speaking your native tongue. Would you prefer I mimic your dialect?" The question was asked in the computer equivalent of posh. It was like being lectured by my father. I shuddered.

"No. Don't do that."

"Of course."

"Can we still destroy that thing with the weapons we have?"

"Unknown."

Brilliant.

"Impact in sixty seconds."

"Do we need to adjust course?"

"If your intention is to impact the Battlestar, no."

"What other intention would I have?"

"Unknown. However, I do not recommend any unnecessary system activations. The Battlestar's technology is much more advanced than the typical Xandraxian Cruiser. They may detect our presence immediately."

"Do they already know we're here?"

"Negative."

"How do you know?" He didn't know anything else.

"We would already be dead."

Dead sounded so very final. I wasn't panicked at the thought, but I realized I did have regrets.

I should have told Darius that I loved him. Should have given him a chance to explain himself. Should have gotten him naked last night instead of pouting in my room like a child.

Too late now.

"Has Dea arrived?"

"Unknown."

Of course Tor didn't know. Dea would have her Titan's

systems shut down as well. We were coming in dark and praying for a miracle.

I looked up at the massive network of black panels connected to make one of the demon star's points. They were coming at me faster than I could comprehend.

Couldn't slow down. One, they'd sense the Titan's power system. Two, space debris didn't slow down. It didn't change course.

I activated my borrowed Titan's grappling claws. Braced myself for pain. The suit I wore would keep me alive, the Titan's internal systems prevent my body from taking most of the impact.

Hitting the massive ship was still going to hurt.

"Impact in three...two...one..."

Make that *miracles*. Plural. I was going to need more than one. And so was Velerion.

 arius, Titan Tycho

I WATCHED Lily climb inside her borrowed Titan and breathed a sigh of relief that she had not sought me out. Well, not me, but Dea, the Starfighter who was supposed to be on this mission.

Dea herself had helped me sneak on board the shuttle in the dark hours of the night. We'd swapped Titans so she could take Intrepidus on her newly assigned mission on Velerion while Tycho and I took her place out here. With Lily. My stubborn, beautiful pair-bonded female.

The launch sequence commenced and the Titan shot off the rail system as fast as I'd ever seen. I stood in the view room and waited until she'd confirmed her coordinates and fired her boosters.

There was no turning back now. For either of us.

She was mine. I was a fool. I'd humiliated her without realizing my mistake. Made her feel that I lacked confidence in her abilities when the opposite was true. She was strong. An excellent fighter. Fearless.

Just like my brother had been.

I was the one who was weak. Afraid to lose her. And yet, my need to keep her safe had driven her from my side, out here, to the most dangerous Titan mission ever attempted.

Somewhere out there were two other shuttles with two Titans on each. Bantia and Ulixes on one. A bonded pair I did not know well on the other. And if any one of our teams failed, Velerion would fall to Queen Raya and the Dark Fleet.

There were few things I was willing to die to protect. Lily was first. But second was my home. My planet. My people. We could not fail.

"Load up, Starfighter. We are approaching your launch coordinates."

I nodded at the shuttle crew member as she walked by and made my way toward Tycho.

After climbing inside, I waited for the rail system to lift me into the launch position. My Titan swayed.

"Starfighter, loading has commenced."

"Copy. Ready to load."

I watched the inner support structures of the launch

bay sway before my eyes. There was no change in gravity, or lack of. The only indication of my movement was the shifting position of the shuttle's walls.

Fighting back the urge to bark at them to hurry the fuck up and get me to Lily, I bit my tongue.

"Launch sequence has commenced. Launch in ten......five, four, three, two, one, launch."

I closed my eyes as my display screens showed streaks of light moving past, the tiny pinpricks of light from distant stars had become lines of white in my peripheral vision.

"Tycho, check out coordinates and launch trajectory. Confirm our position and send it to the shuttle crew."

A few seconds later my Titan responded. "Trajectory confirmed. Ready for booster burn."

"Good luck, Starfighter." The shuttle crew was nothing more than a dot on my monitors now.

"You too. See you on Velerion. Going dark."

Tycho shut down our communications and non-vital systems so we could come up on the Cruiser with as little detectable noise as possible. I wasn't sure this wild scheme of Mia's was going to work, but no one had come up with a better plan and anything was better than sitting on Arturri waiting for Queen Raya's armada to come and destroy our entire civilization.

And then there was Lily. She was out here somewhere. Alone. Angry with me. Hurting. I had done that with my obsessive urge to protect her. I needed to apologize, explain, get her naked and make her come over and over until she gave me another chance.

"Darius? Shall I fire boosters?" Tycho asked. He'd been silently waiting for my command.

"Increase thrust by five percent. I don't want Lily on that Cruiser alone."

"Five percent. Acceptable. However, our reserves will be on the red line."

"Understood." Red line meant I'd be running on luck and prayers if I needed to use them again. Red line was usually good for one adjustment or jump on the ground, but not much else.

I didn't care, as long as I made it to Lily's side, where I belonged.

Tycho fired the booster and I stared out into space for the journey, eyes open but seeing nothing. Thoughts of Lily consumed me. The soft curves of her skin. The way she tangled her fingers in my hair when I pleasured her with my mouth. The hot, wet heat of her clamping down on my cock when she came. The sounds she made.

Her voice. Her smile. The adorable crispness of her speech. She sounded nothing like the other two human females. Her tone was clear. Concise. I loved the way her cheeks turned pink when I teased her. And her obsession with her books.

I'd recovered the two she had placed in the recycling unit. Read every word last night. Had to use my hand to find release more than once as the dominant beasts in her stories claimed their human females. One claiming in particular caught my interest and I fully intended to speak to Lily about it once she was speaking to me again. Allowing me to touch her.

This time, I wouldn't make the same mistakes. She was a Starfighter. An Elite warrior trained to fight to protect Velerion and our people. I could not deny her that power in a bid to keep her safe any more than I could order General Romulus to stop being a general. I'd made peace with that and determined my only course of action going forward.

I would stay by Lily's side. Always. Every mission. We would face every threat, every danger together. And if she died, her life would only be taken once I'd already given mine fighting to protect her.

That was a decision I could live with.

The silence stretched for long hours. Perhaps I dozed off. Perhaps my musings about my female made the time pass quickly, but Tycho alerted me to our arrival a short time later.

"We are five minutes from our destination."

"Copy that. Give me visuals."

A nav grid popped up on my screen and I frowned. Squinted. "You have the wrong vid up, Tycho. Switch to a live camera feed."

"Affirmative. This is the live feed."

What. The. Fuck? This was not possible. "Is that a Dark Fleet Battlestar?"

The nav grid screen shifted and the small black star I'd seen in the center of the screen grew in scope to be equal in size to my face. "Based on the camera evidence, there is a high likelihood that the structure is a Battlestar. Class Seven. Twelve thousand ground troops, four hundred eighty Scythe fighters. Twelve detachable assault towers. That is all the data I have. I cannot confirm that data without scanning the ship. There has never been a Battlestar in the Vega system before."

That, I knew. This was not good.

"Where is Lily?"

"Unknown. Do you want me to activate my scanners?"

"No!" Fuck no. We'd be dead in seconds. This was no half-century old Cruiser from Queen Raya's fleet. That would have been bad enough. This was so much worse. A planet killer. Twelve ships traveling as one designed to break into pieces, surround a planet, block all transmissions, jam all signals in and out as their ship mounted cannons destroyed thousands of targets on the ground below. Followed by ground troop invasion with air support. Of course, they didn't send in their soldiers until there was no resistance left.

"Are we on target?"

"Yes. Impact in two minutes."

"Vega help us. We're in trouble here." I wasn't sure how much Tycho understood about our situation, but I didn't have to tell him to activate our grappling claws or tighten my flight suit in preparation for impact. "Give me a countdown when we're close."

I didn't have long to wait.

"Three. Two. One."

The Titan slammed into the dark black panel near a structural point attaching three of the twelve spikes to the core. I nearly lost consciousness as the force of impact hit me like a boulder in the chest despite Tycho's automatic adjustments. Rather than strike head on, my Titan rolled, the mechanical arms redirecting our armored body in a way to minimize contact as the grappling claws dug deep and slowed us down.

When we finally stopped moving, I held still for several minutes taking stock of our condition. I should be dead. But the engineers, the people who figured things out, built and programmed our Titans, had pulled off a miracle and managed to get my Titan onto this ship without killing me.

I'd buy them all a drink if I made it back alive.

With a groan I felt all the way to my bones, I anchored the grappling claws of my foot deep in the ship's surface and stood to take a look around, engaging the magboots which were designed to keep us from drifting off into space.

I was near the center connecting point for three rising assault towers. Each one black, taller than I could see, and each facet lined with too many energy cannons to get an accurate count. Each of those cannons was easily three times the size of anything I had on the *Resolution.* Compared to this ship, my Titan was like a microbe standing up to inspect a mountain.

"Tycho, are you getting this? General Aryk is going to want every bit of intel we can get him on these ships."

Assuming he was still alive in a few hours. But I kept that thought to myself.

"Confirmed. I am recording and archiving all data."

Well, that was something. "Have you found Lily?"

"Negative."

I had to find her. Now that I knew what she--we--were up against, working as a team was going to be more important than ever.

"Do we have enough firepower to destroy this ship?"

"Negative. However, if the Titan Bellator has retained its full ordnance, the combined force would do significant damage if the charges were strategically placed."

That's what I'd been afraid of. "Hold that thought. I'm going to climb, go to higher ground. Number one priority is locating the Bellator."

"Understood."

Using my Titan's claws, I climbed toward an energy cannon about a third of the way up the structure's side.

"Stop, Darius. I have located the Bellator."

"Where?"

Tycho replaced my forward camera feed with a panoramic view and zoomed in on movement on a neighboring tower. Lily was there, running.

Seconds later, she leaped, propelling herself without grappling hook or claws, toward the core.

"Lily!" What the fuck was she doing?

And then I saw the attack drones chasing her.

"Do we know anything about those drones?" I held on

to my calm by a thread. I had to trust Lily. She'd been right all along.

Tycho changed my view again to focus on the tip of the structure I'd climbed. "Negative. I suspect they are programmed to remove debris and repair the hull should the ship take any damage."

"You're guessing."

"I am. But we will know soon enough."

I looked up to find half a dozen drones closing in. And I'd lost track of Lily.

She was gone.

14

"WHAT THE HELL ARE THESE THINGS?" I kicked two more of the knee-high metallic creatures into deep space like footballs. Didn't matter how many of them I fought off, more appeared as if by magic. And knee high to a Titan? Well, I figured every single one of the things was nearly the size of a show horse.

"Unknown. However, they appear to believe we are debris to be removed from the ship's surface."

"No kidding." I picked one of the repair robot horses and tossed it into space. "Are you sure I can't just smash them?"

"Of course. Destruction or attack would most likely trigger an alarm."

"How do they know I'm not part of the ship?" I bunched the Titan's legs and leaped toward the opposite tower to buy myself some time. Deploying my grappling claw, I pulled myself in until my magboots finished the job of attaching me to the surface of the ship.

I looked back to discover that the robots opposite my location began to disperse. However, when I looked toward the top of my current location, a new swarm had gathered in response to my landing and was headed my way.

"Tor? We need to make these things think we're part of the ship."

"Working on it."

"Work faster."

"I am currently working at maximum capacity. Your request is denied."

"Of course it is." I couldn't help myself. I was beginning to think sarcasm was not limited to humans.

Seconds before this fresh swarm reached me, I leaped again. I couldn't keep this up forever. I needed a plan. And I needed help. "Any sign of Dea?"

"No."

"Of course not."

"That is a very annoying phrase."

"Is it?"

"Of course."

I leaped again, this time down toward one of the main

joints that connected three of the towers. Ships. Points of the demon star, planet destroying monster I had to kill. Perhaps if I could get below the surface the repair robots would ignore me. "Tor, I'm going to crawl down inside. Maybe they'll leave us alone."

"That is dangerous, Lily. Should the ships begin to detach, we will be crushed instantly."

"Got a better idea?"

Tor's silence was deafening.

"Didn't think so."

I ran for the edge of the ship and slid the Titan onto its stomach so I could crawl over the ledge and take a look around. God forbid I jumped into an even worse situation. Not sure how that was possible, but I was ever the eternal optimist.

As my Titan's hips slipped over the rounded corner of the tower, I glanced up at a flicker of movement.

"Tor! See that!" Using the tracking protocols in my helmet, I created a target on the movement. "Enlarge."

I wanted to shout with joy when I recognized the Titan's frame moving toward me.

"That is not Intrepidus."

"What? Then who is it?" I asked, but I already knew.

"Tycho."

"Darius."

Waiting until I was sure he was, indeed, heading for me and not randomly running in my direction, I waved an arm and slipped down below the upper surface of the Battlestar into the ship's joint.

Seconds later, Tycho made the leap from above and jumped down next to me.

"Tor?"

"Your hypothesis was correct. The swarm appears to be confused."

"Thank God."

"Shall I establish direct laser comms with Titan Tycho?"

Was I ready to talk to Darius? Here? Now?

"Yes. Hurry."

"Link established."

Within a blink Darius's face filled my comm screen. His dark hair, worried eyes. I wanted to kiss him. Hug him. Get him in bed and never let him leave.

"Darius?" I knew it was stupid, irrational and completely insane, especially hanging by one of Tor's arms just a meter from the ledge, but I used Tor's free arm to grab Tycho and hug his massive frame.

"Lily? Are you hurt?"

"I'm so sorry. I know you were only trying to protect me. I should have talked to you about it instead of storming off in a rage."

"No. You were right. My behavior was inexcusable. You are powerful, Lily. A warrior. I fell in love with your fearlessness when we were training together. When you chose me, you saved me. And the first thing I tried to do was lock you in a cage."

I was crying now. Damn it. I released my hold on

Tycho but kept Tor close. "What are we going to do? This is not a Cruiser."

On my screen, Darius appeared to be looking around, analyzing the ship. "No, it is not."

"Do you think the other two teams are dealing with a demon star as well?"

"Demon star?" He grinned at me. "I like it."

"I'm serious."

"There's nothing we can do for them. The only thing we can do is complete our mission."

True. Very true. But I was very worried for Bantia and Ulixes and the other team. I didn't know them, other than a brief introduction at the mission briefing, but I felt like we were all in this together. Like somehow, we were cosmically linked. Which was silly and whimsical, but I couldn't make the feeling go away.

"How are we going to destroy this thing? I had Tor run the calculations. We don't have enough explosive firepower to take it out. And the second something goes wrong, this thing will break into pieces and there'll be nothing we can do to stop them."

"I know." Darius closed his eyes. "I'm thinking."

"Apology accepted Darius."

"Yours as well."

"I love you."

His eyes flew open. "Lily."

"Don't say anything. I just needed to tell you, in case..." I looked around the deep crevasse lined with beams and massive panels that could crush us in seconds.

"Do not speak of death. I will not allow it."

"Then we'd better figure something out or we'll be the first of many."

"If I may?" Tor's calm tone interrupted. I had completely forgotten he was here. Which was insane because I was literally riding around inside his Titan body like a baby joey inside a kangaroo's pouch.

"Go ahead, Tor. What do you have for us?" I adored Athena, but I had come to greatly respect Tor's intelligence and experience over the last few hours. Athena was brilliant and new, but Tor had survived things my Titan had not yet imagined.

"I have been inspecting the mechanism by which the twelve satellite ships detach from the core."

"Wait, can Darius hear you?"

"Of course."

"Continue."

If an AI could clear his throat, the odd sound Tor made was the equivalent. "I believe if we can lock four strategically located nodes to lock the ships together for a short time, deploy an initial strike to initiate detachment, and detonate our entire cache of weapons while the joints are under maximum stress, it may be enough to tear their ships to pieces."

"Only four? There are twelve of these spikes." Twelve giant, building sized ships all attached to the center like points on an arrow.

Tycho's voice joined the conversation for the first time

and the familiar sound made me tear up again. "Four joints will suffice."

"Hi Tycho."

"Our Lily. Greetings."

Our Lily? He'd never called me that before. I liked it.

"I have analyzed Tor's plan. I believe he is correct. If we could force the joints to experience extreme torsion prior to detonation, the additional force should be enough to cause hull breaches in each of the twelve attack vessels as well as the core command ship."

Darius's entire demeanor had changed from worried to fierce. Determined. "And this ship is a dodecahedron. Each joint attaches three sections. So, if we make sure we choose one joint for each of the twelve, we will be able to affect all of the attack ships from four centralized locations."

"That is correct."

They'd lost me at dodeca-what? I hated math and geometry. But I was really good at blowing stuff up from inside a Titan. I was even better at mangling metal with my Titan's bare hands. And I wanted to go home. I wanted to survive.

I wanted Darius.

"Let's do this. Tycho. Where do we start."

"This location is as good as any other."

Darius and I turned as one to face the tangled mess of beams and unions that made up the ship's attachment and launch system. "Lead the way."

Tycho placed markers on my nav grid and we made

our way to the first location, a confluence of three massive beams at the central base of three separate attack towers. Each beam came from one side of the giant triangular structure above us.

"Number one?" Darius confirmed.

"Yes. I have marked the towers on your nav grids. This cluster is alpha cluster and this joint is node one."

I looked at my nav grid and studied the display. Tycho had color coded the towers into four sections and marked the one joint the three shared with a pulsing red light on my screen. Four flashing lights. Four places to somehow prevent the ships detaching. And four places to plant bombs.

Now that we had a plan, I was ready to move quickly and get the hell out of here.

I attached my grappling claw to a nearby beam so I wouldn't float away and studied the mess of connections, panels and joints in front of me. "Tell me what to do, Tor. How do we keep this thing from leaving home?"

Selected beams were highlighted on my monitors, as well as arrows indicating areas requiring attention.

"So what do we do? Break them?" I wasn't sure how we were going to do that without alerting the ship to our presence, but we were out of options.

"No. Bend them. Just enough to prevent smooth operation of the rail system." Darius had already moved into position to cover the first mark, Tycho's huge body wrapped around the beam. He braced his legs on the panel below and pulled.

At first, nothing happened. Slowly, I saw movement, a bowing in the center of the beam where Darius had his arms wrapped around it.

"Is that enough?" His strained voice reminded me of the only other time I'd heard him that focused and out of breath. That time, he'd been bending and breaking me into a mess of shattered, orgasmic pieces.

I would never get enough.

"Step back please." Tor waited for Darius to abandon the structure and scanned it again. "Yes. I believe that will create sufficient stress on the joints to increase the impact of our explosives."

"Great. Where's the next one?"

Darius moved to the second beam connected to the central node Tor had chosen as our target. I moved to the third position and pulled. Twisted. Put everything I had into it until my muscles burned.

Tor was a Titan. I didn't know that my extra effort had any effect, but I wasn't about to take any chances.

A few minutes later, Tor gave us the go ahead to attach the bombs we carried. Each placement marked for maximum effect.

"Next?"

A new set of targets appeared on my nav grid. "That's on the other side of the ship."

"Each target is equidistant."

More geometry. "Fine. How are we going to get over there this century without using our boosters?" I glanced down at my grappling claw and the line that ran between the claw to my Titan. "I have an idea."

"Yes, love?"

"Ever play leapfrog when you were a kid?"

"I have never leaped a frog."

I handed the business end of my grappling claw to Tycho and extended the attached line to its maximum length. "Don't let go."

"Never."

With that, I used Tor's mighty strength to propel me through space until the line caught, yanking me to a halt. The force stop caused me to move backward, toward Darius, but I caught a beam and wrapped my arms around it. Legs, too. "Your turn."

"Don't let go."

"Never, Darius. You're mine."

With a running start, Darius leaped forward, his Titan moving toward me at a mind boggling speed. "I shall hold you to that, pair-bond."

He shot past me and I braced for the sharp tug I would feel when he hit the end of the line.

Moments later, it was my turn again, but we'd already covered a significant distance.

"This is going to work."

"Of course it is."

We spent the next few hours leapfrogging past one another all over the enemy ship. I didn't know how close we were to Xenon, or Velerion or the war. But we were moving as quickly as we could and praying Tor's plan would work.

When the last beam was sabotaged and the final charges placed, I heard Darius take a deep breath. "Come on. Hold onto me."

"What the plan?" I asked, moving Tor into Tycho's reach. Darius and I wrapped the Titans' arms around one another. I was not letting go.

"We get the fuck off this ship and pray your friend Mia is as good at her job as everyone says she is."

"She is. I know her. She'll find us."

"You trust her?"

"With my life." I wanted to hold him, skin to skin. Feel his heat. Taste his air. All I could do was stare at his face on a screen. "And yours, Darius. She'll find us."

"All right. Your call. I trust you."

And there they were, the words I'd been waiting to hear my entire life. Even as I smiled with pleasure I realized I didn't need them. Not anymore. I knew who I was and what I was capable of. I didn't need anyone else to tell me what I could or could not do, who I was. What I was worth. I made that decision. No one else.

"I love you."

"You said that before."

"Are you tired of hearing it?"

"No. Never. But I would prefer to have you naked and gasping for air when you say it."

"Of course." I began to see the nearly infinite appeal of Tor's favorite response. So many layers of meaning.

"If you two are finished, I have set the detonation

systems to active. The moment the beams experience increased tension from a detachment event, it will set off a chain reaction. Failing that, I have set a timer on the initial explosive for ten minutes to initiate the event. We need to go," Tor said.

"Copy that." Darius looked at me, or rather, directly into his screen. "Ready?"

"Always."

"Magboots off and maximum jump in three...two...one...jump!"

Tycho and Tor took care of deactivating our magboots as we used every ounce of power our Titans' possessed to leap away from the ship and into space.

Clinging to one another, we floated away as the Battlestar continued on its journey. "Do you think the others made it?"

"Yes."

"I think so, too." I had a good feeling about this. If we had figured out a solution, I had to have faith that the other Elite Starfighters had a well.

"Lily?"

"Yes?"

"I read your books last night."

Oh. My. God. "I threw those away."

"I knew they were important to you. I retrieved them."

"And you read them? Why?"

"I was trying to understand where I'd gone wrong. What you needed."

Oh shit. "I don't need an Atlan beast, Darius. Not when I have you."

"I'll make sure of that."

"So? Why are you telling me this now?"

"There was one part of the story in particular that I feel I must ask about."

"What part?"

"Do you like chocolate cake and cherry cheesecake?"

Holy shit. He really *did* read them. "Do you even have chocolate on Velerion? Or cherries?"

"I will find a way to acquire some. I would very much like to do as this Rezzer did and taste your favorite sweets directly from your skin. And your pussy."

Was it hot in here? What was I supposed to say?

Say yes, stupid.

"Okay. Yes. I'd like that."

"Excellent."

I'd like him to tell me he loved me as well, but I could wait. I didn't need external validation. Not anymore. I could love him and not worry about anything else.

The feeling was damn liberating.

We floated silently for what felt like hours but was only a few minutes before Tor's voice interrupted my imaginings of Darius licking chocolate frosting off my nipples and cherry syrup from my...

"Detonation in five seconds. Four. Three. Two. One."

The blast was small. Disappointing. More like a tiny flicker of light than an explosion.

"That was anticlimactic," I said.

"Wait for it," Darius said and I bit the inside of my cheek as Tor enlarged our view of the enemy ship.

At first nothing happened. There was no sound in space, but I imagined I could hear the bent beams of the ship's rail systems squeaking and groaning with strain as the massive ship attempted to break apart in response to the explosion. They would believe they were under attack.

Nothing.

"Are you sure they will separate, Tor? That wasn't a small bomb and a really big ship."

"Tower separation is standard operating procedure for Battlestars under attack."

I really, really hoped he was right.

The first sign of trouble was a small flash near the core. Then another. Another.

I squealed with glee as the ship lit up like a string of flashing christmas tree lights and the pieces, the towers, detached, spewing fire and atmosphere that propelled them in random, uncontrollable directions.

Two collided. The burst of light made me close my eyes.

The shockwave rolled over us, shooting us deeper into space faster even than the rail launcher inside the Velerion shuttles.

Darius and I clung to one another, all smiles.

"It worked," I said.

"Of course," Tor replied.

No doubt about it, this time he was absolutely being smug.

Now, for that rescue Mia had promised. We were moving fast, in the wrong direction in the middle of a massive field of debris from that Battlestar.

"How much air do you have left?" I asked.

"Enough."

"Damn it, Darius. Stop trying to protect me." I was down to less than twenty minutes.

"Ten minutes. Maybe fifteen."

"Tor, link your air supply to Tycho's."

"Lily, no!"

"Don't argue! If you die, we both die. Got it? We are either in this thing together or we're not. You can't treat me like a child. I am a Starfighter, Darius. Just like you."

"No. You are not like me, my Lily. You are far superior and always will be."

"Good. Then stop arguing. Tor?"

"Already done, Lily."

"Thank you." I tried to remain calm, preserve the air supply. Panicking wouldn't help. I'd taken SCUBA training and knew the worst thing I could do was panic. "Come on, Mia. Come. On!"

"I love you, Lily."

"Shut up. Just shut up. We are not going to die out here."

Darius laughed and the sound had me smiling back at him. "I love you, too. And you are not dying on me. I want that chocolate and cheesecake."

"There was another. A male named Dare. Very similar to my name, although he and his mate wore a strange collar. He restrained his mate so he could enjoy tasting her core for an extended period of time without interference."

If I didn't suffocate from lack of oxygen, I might burn alive from Darius's new knowledge from the contents of my romance novels.

Perhaps I wouldn't hunt down the author if I ever returned to Earth. Maybe, I'd thank her instead. Hot, sexy aliens really *did* exist. And this one was mine.

"Mia! Where are you?"

Tor's calm tone made me jump. I'd forgotten about him. Again.

"I have reactivated our communications and scanners. A Velerion shuttle is closing in on our location now. Estimated arrival in fifteen minutes."

"That's not fast enough."

Darius was right. We wouldn't last that long.

"Tor, we still have some juice in the boosters?"

"Yes. Very little. Less than five percent."

"Get us five percent closer to that shuttle."

"Of course."

15

ily, Moon Base Arturri, Three Days Later

WE WERE ALIVE. We were naked. The other Titan teams had been successful and the Dark Fleet had officially withdrawn their support of Queen Raya's claim on the Vega system.

The war had taken a turn in our favor. For the first time since Queen Raya's initial attack, Velerion was *winning.*

They'd given me a medal. Darius, too. I felt like a peacock at the zoo when they lined up the three Earth women along with their Starfighter men and hung medallions the size of dinner plates around our necks. I was shocked when a man in a robe--he looked more like a

monk than a politician--proudly announced that at least
a dozen additional humans had nearly completed the
training simulations. Twelve more earthlings would soon
be on their way. He didn't specify if the new Starfighters
were male or female, where they were from. Their age.

None of that mattered if they knew how to fight, or fly,
or hack into enemy ship systems.

The leaders of Velerion had given the training simulation designers medallions as well. I'd once believed
computer nerds were the same the universe over. But no.
These programmers, engineers and designers were hot.
Even the women, and I didn't normally pay attention to
women.

Everyone was chuffed. They gave us our medals,
hosted a feast followed by a dance--I knew zero steps,
depending on Darius to carry me around the room--and
continually requested support from the obviously influ-
ential or wealthy Velerions in attendance.

Seemed pomp, circumstance and ass kissing was a
thing everywhere.

I didn't care about the shiny swirl shapes Darius had
insisted we hang on our wall. It was the Starfighter
emblem and matched the dark swirls we each had on our
necks. That was what I cared about. I had the prize I
wanted.

Him.

I sat on the edge of our bed and reached for him. He
knelt on the floor before me, our faces almost perfectly

aligned. Darius leaned forward and cupped my jaw. "I will not be gentle. I need you."

He kissed me then, softly, so sweetly that his words took longer than they should have to register.

Did I want him to be gentle? Sometimes. But not right now. Right now I needed wild and rough and desperate. This was the first time we'd been truly alone in our own space since returning from the mission.

I DIDN'T WANT soft or slow. I wanted him to fuck my brains out and make me forget my own name. I wanted to be reduced to animal lust. Mindless. Consuming.

I wanted him to lose himself in pleasure, sink into my body and never want to leave.

The thought made my pussy clench. God, yes, I wanted him to claim me. Mark me. I wanted my fingernails to leave marks on his skin so no other woman would dare think about taking what was mine. I wanted to feel possessed. Worshiped. Loved. I wanted to close my eyes and give him everything. "I don't want gentle. I need you, too."

With a moan that sounded like pain Darius crushed his lips to mine, his tongue teasing and tasting me as if he would never get enough.

I felt his huge hands reach up and around me to the back of my neck, holding me in place for his kiss, his possession.

When I was panting and weak, he pulled his lips from mine. "Lay down on the bed. Face down. I want to play."

Eager to see what he had in mind, I climbed onto the bed and settled on my stomach.

"Spread your legs, Lily. Let me see what's mine."

Oh, god. I knew this part of the story. I'd probably read it at least a dozen times. And I knew I wasn't supposed to obey him fast enough. Knew what was coming...

As expected, a sharp smack landed on my bare bottom. The sting spread like wildfire and I gasped as the heat reached my core. As instructed, I moved my thighs a bit farther apart, but Darius, as per the role he was playing in our game, used both hands to push my knees wide. He took a large pillow from the pile near the head of the bed and lifted my hips to slide the pillow beneath me.

I fought back a low moan as I tried to imagine what we looked like. Together. Him hard and ready behind me, poised to plunder and take and show no mercy.

I understood how Hannah felt in the book. Like her, I was completely at his mercy. My ass was up in the air, displayed in the brightly lit room. My pussy was open and waiting. Hungry for him. The cool air in the room did nothing to lessen the heat.

"So pretty, Lily. So wet. Swollen. Are you sensitive?" Darius rubbed my ass cheeks with both hands, pulling hard enough to put my core on display. His fingers swiped through the wetness but denied me relief. He teased me as my body heated everywhere he touched.

Two large fingers slipped inside me and I cried out at the invasion. "Who is your master now, mate?" He finger fucked me until I moaned and pushed back against his hand. "Your pussy is so wet I could fuck you right now, take you hard and fast and you'd beg me for more."

"Yes." Fuck. Me. How did he remember exactly what to say?

He didn't hurt me, but he wasn't gentle. I felt the moment my inner muscles opened for him. He slid three fingers deep and fast in a rush of pleasure-pain that tore a moan from my throat. Darius moved his fingers inside me, shifting them back and forth gently, not fucking me, but teasing me, playing with me, exploring me. He pushed me to the edge of sanity until I knew I would beg him to do more. Do more. Take more. Take anything he wanted.

His hand landed on my ass with a sharp sting and I yelped.

"That was for leaving me, Lily. For denying your need for me. For denying my right to protect you."

Oh, this role-playing game was getting a little too real. "I don't need you to protect me."

He leaned close, his chest covering my back, and whispered in my ear. "I know you do not need my protection, love. But it's my right to do everything I can to keep you safe. You will not deny me again. Leave me behind. Choose another to be at your side."

I'd hurt him by going off with Dea instead of choosing him. I realized that now. Hurt him deeply.

"I'm sorry." I didn't hide my emotions or my needs. I loved him. I was who I was and he had accepted that. "I love you. I won't leave you behind. Ever. Please." I needed release. Pleasure. I needed *him.*

The tension in my body was so high even the soft bedding rubbing my skin was too much. Overwhelming. Almost painful.

"You're sorry? Aren't you forgetting something?" He pulled his hard length free and replaced them with two fingers as his other hand landed with a sharp sting on my other cheek.

Forgetting? God, what was I forgetting? "What?" I cried.

He struck my bottom again, spanking me as I'd asked, as some of the heroes in my erotic novels were wont to do.

I didn't know if I would like it, but we were playing a game.

And that sting on my bottom was shockingly heated. The sting spreading like fire all over my body.

Darius rubbed my bare ass as his thumb found my clit and rubbed back and forth slowly. Too slow. I needed stimulation to have an orgasm, not this. I wiggled my hips, trying to force him to move, and his palm landed again. "Lily, when we are in our private quarters, you will call me master or sir. Do you understand?"

Oh, shit. That was a line straight out of the book.

How could I have forgotten? It had been my idea to play this game. We'd read the scene together. He was playing the part of a Prillon warrior, Dare. I was Hannah. We didn't have collars on, and I had made very clear I was not ready to try anything via the backdoor, yet...but this? Pretending to be someone else?

I felt free. Totally, completely free to say anything. Do anything. "Yes, *sir*."

Surrender. Submission. I trusted him completely, which was not just shocking but a joy I'd never expected to experience in real life.

I called him *sir*.

Damn, that was hot.

In a move so fast I gasped in shock, I was flipped onto my back and he towered over me. Darius lifted my arms over my head and held them, stared down into my eyes. "Hold your arms over your head and keep them there."

I did as he commanded and felt consumed as he stared into my eyes as he worked me with his hand, bringing me to the brink over and over. Watching every move. Every reaction. Stopping just as the wave of an orgams was about to roar through me. Over and over until I was thrashing on the bed, nearly in tears. "Do you want to come, Lily?"

"Yes."

"Yes, what?" His hand stilled and I whimpered. One hard stroke, the thickness of his body claiming mine. One thing. Just one more thing would push me over the edge. I was strung so tight I felt like I was going to explode.

"Yes, *sir*."

His smile almost made me come. I felt powerful. I'd pleased him, and the heated emotions flooding my body had nothing to do with sex and everything to do with giving him what he wanted. What he needed. He was mine.

"Beg, Lily. Say please."

"Please, sir. Please." I was desperate and I hid nothing.

Darius lowered his mouth to mine and used his tongue in my mouth to mimic the movements of his hand below.

The orgasm ripped through me like an explosion. I cried out, my entire body lifting from the bed with the force of my release. His kiss stole my air, gave it back.

I shuddered in his arms as he kissed his way down my body and took my pussy with his mouth. He sucked and licked my clit, using his fingers to stroke me inside until I came apart again.

"Darius. Now. I need you inside me."

I couldn't resist when he moved to cover me. I tangled my fingers in his hair and pulled him close. Devoured him with my kiss. Lifted my hips to take him deep.

It only took a few seconds before he lost himself. He held me in place, pinned between the bed and his large body, thrusting hard and fast. Deep.

My body responded instantly, my throbbing core pulsing around him as another release rolled over me.

"I love you, Lily." He pushed deep, kept the orgasm a fire in my body. Pushed me to respond.

His words broke me and my body followed my heart over another cliff. This time the release was softer. Gentle. It was as if my body knew this time was meant to be different. This wasn't just sex, this was love. Making love.

I'd never done it before.

His kiss changed from demanding to gentle, his touch from aggressive to tender and I had no will to do anything but stay where he wanted me, to allow him to worship and claim me. His release came soon after, his entire body rigid as he sighed my name over and over. His lips left mine to trace a path along my neck. Back up again. He stayed inside me where we both wanted him and kissed me. Over and over until I knew I'd never get the taste of him out of my mouth. I didn't move. I couldn't. I had nothing left.

"Lily, my Lily."

"Yes?" My response was more sigh than anything else. I would not move, not so long as he wanted me here.

"You are mine, my everything. I love you."

"I love you, too."

"Didn't you forget something?" He used his commanding tone and I smiled, brushing a strand of hair from the forehead of the man I adored.

"I love you, *sir.*"

"That's more like it." Darius rolled onto his back with a happy smile and brought me with him, tucking me neatly into his side. I sighed with contentment when he pulled up the bedding to cover us both.

"I could get used to this."

"Now you want to be a Prillon warrior?"

He grinned and kissed the top of my head. "I shall reserve judgment until my special order from Earth has arrived."

"Special order?"

"Chocolate cake and cherry cheesecake. Don't tell me you forgot."

Oh god. I didn't think it was possible, but my core fluttered back to life.

"Are you going to limit yourself to one word commands when you go into beast mode?"

Darius laughed. "Depends how much I like chocolate."

Good lord, I'd created a monster.

My monster.

I curled into his side, safe and warm and content, and I trusted Darius to watch over me. Protect me.

Now. And always.

EPILOGUE

*I*n a secure location aboard her battleship, Queen Raya watched the captain of her guard approach. He was massive. Scarred. Cruel.

He was her favorite, both in battle and in bed.

"My queen, the ambassador has arrived."

"Bring them to me."

"Yes, my queen." The large warrior bowed and left her in peace.

The throne room was quiet. Her heart was not.

The Dark Fleet had proven themselves to be cowards, running because they'd lost three ships.

Three.

Raya had lost thousands.

EPILOGUE

*W*ant to read the book Lily took with her to Velerion? Read Chapter One of *Interstellar Brides® Program: The Colony:* Her Cyborg Beast NOW!

CHAPTER ONE:

CJ, Interstellar Bride Processing Center, Miami, Florida

"I STAND. NO BED." A deep, rumbling voice filled my head. My mind. My body. This body knew that voice. Knew it and shivered in anticipation. Somehow I knew this male was mine. He was huge. Not in his normal state. He had some kind of sickness. A fever that would cause him to go insane if I didn't tame him. Fuck him. Make him mine forever.

I felt the softness of a bed at my back—my *naked* back —and then I was hoisted up as if I weighed nothing. That was a joke because I weighed plenty. I wasn't a tiny waif or a Victoria's Secret model. Well, I was tall like one, just over six feet, but I had boobs and hips. Strong hands banded about my waist, spun me about so my back was pressed to his front. His *naked* front. Hands slid up and cupped my breasts.

Oh.

Wow.

Um.

Yes. God, yes.

This was crazy. Completely crazy. I didn't like to be manhandled. Hell, I did the manhandling. I ate weak men for breakfast and made stronger ones cry by lunchtime. All in a day's work.

But I wasn't at work now.

I had no idea where the hell I was, but this guy knew just how to push every one of my hot buttons. Or should I say, *her* hot buttons. I wasn't me. Well, I was here, but this wasn't me. The thoughts going through my head, the knowledge, wasn't mine. But the reactions? One tug on my nipples and my pussy was wet and aching. Empty.

I felt the hot throb of his cock against my back. He was tall, really tall based on how far down the bed was from me now. Yet his hands cupped all of my breasts.

They usually were overflowing. Triple Ds tended to do that, but not with him. Nope.

I felt...small.

But, this wasn't me. Was it?

It *felt* like me.

"Better," he growled, walking us both slowly toward a table. We were in some kind of room, sterile and impersonal, like a hotel room with a big bed, table and chairs. I couldn't see much else, but I wasn't looking because as soon as my thighs bumped into the cool edge of the table, he leaned forward, forcing me down over the top. I resisted. "Down, mate."

Mate?

I bristled at the firm hand pushing me down, at his commanding tone. That word. I wasn't anyone's mate. I didn't date. I fucked, sure, but I was the one to walk away. I was the one on top, in control. But now? I had zero control, and it was uncomfortable. But the need to let go, to let this guy take over? I wanted it. Well, my pussy did. My nipples did, too. And the woman whose body I inhabited, she wanted it, too. But unlike me, she wasn't afraid. She didn't fight this, or him.

She resisted because she knew he wanted her to. Knew it would make his cock hard and his pulse race. Knew it would push him to the edge of control. She wanted to make sure that when it came to control, she had none. The thought of the cuffs—cuffs?—she knew were coming made her pussy clench with heat.

Which was just damn weird to me, but there was

nothing I could do about it. I was a witness and partici-pant, but I wasn't really here. I felt like a ghost inside her body, living someone else's fantasy.

Hot fantasy, sure. But not real. This wasn't real.

This body was all about letting the big brute do anything he wanted. My mind had other ideas. But I had no control here. This body wasn't mine. The thoughts going through my head weren't mine either. This woman —me—whoever I was right now—wanted to push him. She wanted to be dominated. She wanted to be conquered. Controlled. Fucked until she screamed. And I was simply along for the ride. "I don't like to be bossed around," she/I said.

"Liar." I saw a big hand settle onto the table beside me, saw the blunt fingers, the scars, the dusting of hair on the wrist. Felt the other big hand pressing into my back. Harder. More insistent.

I hissed when my breasts came in contact with the hard surface, and I put my elbows out to keep from being lowered all the way, but he changed tactics, his hand moving from my back to my pussy, two fingers sliding deep. "Wet. Mine."

I felt the broad expanse of his torso against my back, his skin hot, the hard length of his cock rubbing along my wet slit, teasing. And he was right. I was wet. Hot. So eager for him I was afraid this crazy woman—whose body I currently inhabited—was going to break down and *beg. Beg!*

His lips brushed along my spine, fingers slid my hair

to the side, and his kisses continued along my neck as his hands worked their magic. One pressing me slowly, inevitably toward a prone position on the table. The other rubbed my bare bottom, huge fingers dipping toward my core, sliding deep, retreating to stroke my sensitive bottom again in a repetitive tease that made me squirm.

The gesture was gentle, reverent even, and completely at odds with his dominance. Two metal bracelets came into my view as he set them down in front of me. Silver toned, they were thick and wide, with decorative etchings in them.

The sight made me hotter, the woman's reaction nearly orgasmic. She wanted them on her wrists, heavy and permanent. They would mark her as his mate. Forever.

I had no idea where they came from, but my mind wasn't working properly, and I couldn't figure it out. Not with the soft lips, the flick of his tongue, the prodding of his cock over my slick folds and the rush of longing filling me.

The bracelets looked old and matched ones that were already on his wrists. I hadn't noticed them before now, but that didn't surprise me.

He shifted, opening one and putting it on my wrist, then the other. Even though I was pressed into the table by his formidable body, I didn't feel threatened. It felt like he was giving me a gift of some kind, something precious.

I just had no idea what.

"They're beautiful," I heard myself say.

He growled again, the rumbling of it vibrating from his chest and into my back. "Mine. Bad girl. Fuck now."

I had no idea why I'd be a bad girl, especially if his cock was as big as it felt. I wanted it.

"Yes. Do it!" I spread my legs wider, not sure what he expected, but knowing I didn't care. I wanted him to fuck me now. I didn't want to be good. I wanted to be bad. Very, very bad.

Evidently, I'd lost my mind because I had no idea what he looked like. Who he was. Where I was. But none of that mattered. And why did the idea of being manhandled or even spanked appeal like it never had before?

He shifted his hips, slid his cock over my folds, and it settled at my entrance. I felt the broad head, so big that it parted my slick lips, and as he pressed in, I whimpered.

He was huge. Like enormous. He was careful as he filled me, as if he knew he might be too much.

I shifted my hips, tried to take him, but my inner walls clenched and squeezed, tried to adjust. My hands couldn't find purchase on the smooth surface, and I lowered myself down, put my cheek against the wood, angling my hips up.

He slid in a touch farther.

I gasped, shook my head. "Too big." My voice was soft, breathy. He wasn't. He'd fit. He might hurt me, might shock me, but I wanted him. Every damn inch.

"Shh," he crooned.

From nowhere, a memory surfaced of this male

speaking to me when I'd been worried about this moment. His beast—what was a beast?—*You can take a beast's cock. You were made for it. You were made for me.*

As he slid in to the hilt and I felt his hips press against my bottom, I had to agree with him. I was milking him and clenching down, adjusting to being filled so much, but it felt good.

God, did it ever.

"Ready, mate?"

Ready? For what? He was already in.

But when he pulled back all the way so my folds clung to him before he plunged deep, I realized I hadn't been ready.

The pounding stole the breath from my lungs, but I almost came. I had no idea how because I'd never come from just vaginal penetration only. I needed to rub my clit with my own fingers.

When he did it again, I realized fingers were definitely not needed.

"Yes!" I cried. I couldn't help it. I wanted it. Needed it. I shimmied, pressed back as he plunged in once more.

His hand moved, gripped my wrists, held onto the bracelets.

He held me down and fucked me.

There was no escape. No reprieve. No stopping him as the orgasm built into a dangerous thing. And I wanted all of it. I wanted *him*.

"Come. Now. Scream. I fill you up."

He was a dirty talker, too. Not much for complete sentences, but that was part of his charm.

I was so drenched for him I could hear the wet slap of our bodies as he pounded into me. I could feel the wet coating in the cool air, slipping from me and down my thighs.

Holding me down with one hand, he grabbed my bottom with the other, a full lobe in his grasp, pulling me open. Wider.

He pushed deeper. Harder. I thrashed on the table, both excited and vulnerable, stretched out before him. Unable to move. Unable to resist. I had to accept whatever he wanted to give me. Trust. Surrender.

The thought made me groan, my body spiraling ever higher as I fought, holding back my final fall.

He released my bottom, a single sharp spank landing like liquid heat on my bare skin. And that orgasm he commanded from me? The one I was holding back? Yeah, there it was. I screamed, arched my back, my hard nipples chafing against the table top as I lost control, went blind, an abyss opening up to swallow me as I shattered.

I lost all sense of myself, my only reality the hard thrust of his cock as he pumped into me as my pussy milked him.

"Mate," he said, just before he sank deep, settled, then roared like an animal.

It was like a beast had filled him, taken over. Claimed me.

I felt his seed, hot and thick, coating me deep inside.

It was too much for me to hold as he moved again, fucking me through his release, his hot seed sliding from me and down my thighs.

I felt so good and so wrong. Controlled. Overpowered. Blatantly claimed.

Bad. Bad. Bad. I was soooo bad right now.

I didn't even try to get up, not even when he released my wrists and grabbed my hips to pull me back. Hard. He lifted my ass off the table and pulled me onto his cock which was already swelling. Ready for more.

I groaned, trying to move my arms. No luck, but something rattled. The sound odd. Out of place.

"Stay." He grunted the order and thrust into me again. Submitting to him went against everything I was, and yet...my pussy clenched with his barked command. Perhaps I wasn't everything I imagined.

His fingers dug deep, pulling me back until he bottomed out inside me.

Yes!

I was hot all over again. Ready for more. Needy. I could go for hours...

"Caroline." The voice came from out of nowhere. Cold. Clinical. A woman's voice.

Who?

Everything faded even as I struggled to stay in that body, as he pulled out and slowly filled me again. Spread me open. I groaned, fighting for it. Fighting to stay with him.

"Caroline!" Sharp this time. Insistent. Like a teacher scolding her student.

Oh God. The testing...

I gasped—this time not from pleasure—and my eyes flew open.

Instead of bracelets about my wrists, I had restraints. I was naked, but I wasn't bent over with my lover's hands on my hips. I was shackled to a medical exam chair wearing an Interstellar Brides Processing Center gown. The logo tracked up and down the hospital-style gown in neat, perfect rows of burgundy on gray fabric.

Clinical. Sterile. All business.

I wasn't pressed over a hard table. I wasn't being filled and fucked until my entire body exploded. There was no giant man.

There was only me and a stern looking woman in her late twenties. Gray eyes. Dark brown hair coiled tightly into a bun at the base of her skull. She looked like a grumpy ballerina, and her name floated to the surface even before I read her name tag.

Warden Egara. She was doing my testing. Testing for the Interstellar Brides Program. A process which would match me to an alien and send me into outer space to be his wife.

Forever.

INTERSTELLAR BRIDES® PROGRAM: *The Colony:* Her Cyborg Beast NOW!

A SPECIAL THANK YOU TO MY READERS...

Want more? I've got *hidden* bonus content on my web site *exclusively* for those on my mailing list.

If you are already on my email list, you don't need to do a thing! Simply scroll to the bottom of my newsletter emails and click on the *super-secret* link.

Not a member? What are you waiting for? In addition to ALL of my bonus content (great new stuff will be added regularly) you will be the first to hear about my newest release the second it hits the stores—AND you will get a free book as a special welcome gift.

Sign up now! http://freescifiromance.com

FIND YOUR INTERSTELLAR MATCH!

YOUR mate is out there. Take the test today and discover your perfect match. Are you ready for a sexy alien mate (or two)?

VOLUNTEER NOW!

interstellarbridesprogram.com

DO YOU LOVE AUDIOBOOKS?

Grace Goodwin's books are now available as
audiobooks...everywhere.

LET'S TALK!

Interested in joining my **Sci-Fi Squad**? Meet new like-minded sci-fi romance fanatics and chat with Grace! Get excerpts, cover reveals and sneak peeks before anyone else. Be part of a private Facebook group that shares pictures and fun news! Join here:

https://www.facebook.com/groups/scifisquad/

Want to talk about Grace Goodwin books with others? Join the **SPOILER ROOM** and spoil away! Your GG BFFs are waiting! (And so is Grace) Join here:

https://www.facebook.com/groups/ggspoilerroom/

GET A FREE BOOK!

http://freescifiromance.com

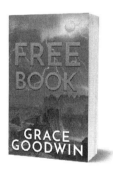

Interstellar Brides® Program: The Colony

Her Cyborg Warriors

The Colony Boxed Set 1

The Colony Boxed Set 2

Interstellar Brides® Program: The Virgins

The Alien's Mate

His Virgin Mate

Claiming His Virgin

His Virgin Bride

His Virgin Princess

The Virgins - Complete Boxed Set

Interstellar Brides® Program: Ascension Saga

Ascension Saga, book 1

Ascension Saga, book 2

Ascension Saga, book 3

Trinity: Ascension Saga - Volume 1

Ascension Saga, book 4

Ascension Saga, book 5

Ascension Saga, book 6

Faith: Ascension Saga - Volume 2

Ascension Saga, book 7

Ascension Saga, book 8

Ascension Saga, book 9

Destiny: Ascension Saga - Volume 3

Other Books

Their Conquered Bride

Wild Wolf Claiming: A Howl's Romance

ABOUT GRACE

Grace Goodwin is a USA Today and international best-selling author of Sci-Fi and Paranormal romance with more than one million books sold. Grace's titles are available worldwide in multiple languages in ebook, print and audio formats. Two best friends, one left-brained, the other right-brained, make up the award winning writing duo that is Grace Goodwin. They are both mothers, escape room enthusiasts, avid readers and intrepid defenders of their preferred beverages. (There may or may not be an ongoing tea vs. coffee war occurring during their daily communications.) Grace loves to hear from readers! All of Grace's books can be read as sexy, stand-alone adventures. But be careful, she likes her heroes hot and her love scenes hotter. You have been warned...

www.gracegoodwin.com
gracegoodwinauthor@gmail.com

Printed in Great Britain
by Amazon

65989019R00111